"YOU CAN'T ARREST ME. I'M THE SHERIFF!"

Longarm said grimly, "Better I lock you up than the people of this county string you up."

"Whatever in the world are you talkin' about?"

"Listen, Otis . . . You been getting away with murder for several years because that bunch of cutthroats you been harboring within the confines of Mason County have done all their robbing in other places. But now they have put you in a pretty fix by robbing the auction barn. They didn't rob Mr. Ownsby and his wife. They robbed the folks that have been dumb enough to vote for you. Maybe you are so damned ignorant you couldn't see just how riled up that crowd was. They blame you, Bodenheimer. And as soon as they find out you were on the other side of the county on a wild-goose chase and that you lured me out there, they are going to be fit to be tied. Except that ain't what I think they'll do with the rope." Longarm stood up, though he did not draw his revolver. All five men standing there took an instinctive step backward.

"You're a crook, Bodenheimer. There's two things that smell awful when they go bad, and dead fish is one of them. The other one is crooked law. I can't stand the smell of either one. So I'm going to put you in a jail cell until I get this mess straightened out. Now put your damn gunbelts on top of this desk. *Now!*"

◆► TABOR EVANS ◄◆

LONGARM

**AND THE
DAUGHTERS OF DEATH**

J

JOVE BOOKS, NEW YORK

LONGARM AND THE DAUGHTERS OF DEATH

A Jove Book / published by arrangement with
the author

PRINTING HISTORY
Jove edition / January 1996

ISBN: 0-515-11783-8

A JOVE BOOK®
Jove Books are published by The Berkley Publishing Group,
200 Madison Avenue, New York, New York 10016.
JOVE and the "J" design are trademarks
belonging to Jove Publications, Inc.

PRINTED IN THE UNITED STATES OF AMERICA

10 9 8 7 6 5 4 3 2 1

Chapter 1

Longarm almost had the young woman completely undressed. He'd gotten her blouse and skirt off and her slip and chemise. Now she stood in the middle of the room of the little cabin wearing only her bloomers and her little leather slippers. He was down on his knees in front of her, his breath starting to come too fast to make breathing comfortable, getting ready to ease her feet out of the slippers and then go to work on the bloomers. She stood there, naked from the waist up, her beautiful young milk-white breasts erect and topped with cherry-colored nipples pointing at him like twin cannons.

There came a pounding on the cabin door and a voice called out, "Marshal, Marshal Long! You got to come quick!"

Longarm sighed and stood up, looking at the girl regretfully. It was fortunate that the call had come when it did, but it was damned bad luck that it had come at all. He had not undressed other than to take off his hat and his gunbelt. Now he picked his gunbelt up off the floor and buckled it around his waist, still enjoying the sight of the girl. Hannah was her name, Hannah Diver. He reflected, as he took her by the arm and steered her toward the bed, that he would have liked to have done some diving on her. She walked like a sleepwalker, moving docilely and easily at his touch. Diver wasn't really her last name. Six weeks before she'd married a man named Gus Horne, but an hour after her marriage, Gus had been called away by the gang of outlaws he worked with, and she was still waiting to have her marriage consummated. Longarm, after a week of diligent preparation, had been just about to handle the job for her. If she acted like she was sleeping on her feet or in a trance, it was because she was still a bit apprehensive at the prospect of what was about to happen to her. In everyday life, and in a familiar activity, she was something of a spitfire, as Longarm had reason to know.

Now he bade her get in the bed. He helped her under the covers and assured her he wouldn't be long. She turned her head on the pillow and looked up at him with eyes that hinted at fire and said, "That's what Gus told me, an' I been keeping myself Sunday-clean and perfumed for damn near two months, and what has it got me?"

He leaned down and kissed her as the pounding started on the cabin door again. He said, a little pain in his groin, "I promise, Hannah. Let me get rid of whoever is at the door and I will be right back. But you stay under the covers so you don't have to get dressed again." Before he moved, he lifted the covers to look at her firm, thrusting breasts again. It was a little cool in the cabin, and her nipples were puckered and hard. He ran his eyes down what he could see of her, all the way from her light brown hair and hazel eyes to the small waist and the tops of her perfectly rounded thighs. He sighed. The pounding was still coming at the door. He didn't often get a chance to do a good turn for such a delicious-looking twenty-two-year-old maiden in distress, and he hated like hell to leave his work unfinished. He dropped the covers, told Hannah he wouldn't be but

2

a moment, and then walked across the hardwood floor of the big cabin.

He took hold of the wrought-iron handle, tripped the latch, and jerked open the heavy wooden door. A man, considerably smaller than Longarm's six-foot, 190-pound frame, stood there, his fist still poised in the air to knock again. He had a deputy sheriff's badge on his shirt and a weak, ferret-like look on his face.

Longarm said, letting his irritation show, "What the hell you want? Don't you know I'm in here interviewing the wife of one of the culprits? What's the matter with you, Deputy Purliss? Ain't you got a damn lick of sense, interrupting an interview like this?"

Purliss always sounded as if he was struggling to catch his breath. He said, "I'm mighty sorry, Marshal Long, but the sheriff done told me to fetch you. They got them boys treed 'bout six miles up river. Got 'em penned up in a cave, way up on the bluff. Sheriff wants you to come."

With a sigh Longarm stepped out of the cabin and shut the door behind him. He said, "Purliss, the sheriff has had that gang treed, as you call it, before and it came to nothing. Now, I am getting damn tired of his wild-goose chases. Especially now when I am about to get some information out of Gus Horne's wife."

"But they is there, Marshal. An' Sheriff Bodenheimer wants you to come. There is some question they is across the county line an' he wouldn't have jurs'diction, don't you know. So he needs you, you bein' a federal officer an' all."

Longarm frowned. "How many damn times I got to explain to Bodenheimer that it don't matter about county lines if he is in hot pursuit."

"But that be the thang, Marshal. Sheriff Bodenheimer ain't shore he could be considered in hot pursuit an' he don't want to get it all screwed up that he was out his jurs'diction."

3

Longarm looked off in the distance and shook his head. Otis Bodenheimer was nearly the dumbest man, let alone lawman, that he'd ever met. The sheriff was an overweight, pear-shaped cuss with a jug butt and nothing between the ears. His only saving feature was that he was kin to half the voters in Mason County, who would rather elect him to sheriff every two years than have to take care of him and his family. As a consequence they got the best law enforcement that charity could buy. Longarm said to Purliss, "You say they are about six miles up the river?"

"Yessir, yessir. We are to come quick as we can."

The handsome little cabin was set along the banks of the Llano River, a clear, cool stream that cut through the rough hill country of southwest Texas. It was two miles outside of Mason, Texas, the county seat of Mason County. Longarm had been there a little over a week and it was, to his mind, the damnedest job of work he'd been sent on since he had joined the federal Marshals' Service some fifteen years past. For at least two years, requests and pleas for help had been coming into the offices of the Marshals' Service by various means, all of them complaining about a gang of outlaws who operated out of a small county some one hundred miles southwest of the Texas capital in Austin. Either through connivance with local lawmen, or because of the incompetence of the sheriff in Mason County, the gang couldn't seem to be caught or broken up. They would dash out of Mason County, commit some depredation, and then hurry back to their hideout, thought to be somewhere near the town of Mason. The gang was described as having as many as ten members or as few as six, depending on who was telling the story. Since the Denver district office was the closest to the area, the requests for help had come there to Chief Marshal Billy Vail. For the most part the complaints about the gang had been ignored. There was too much work as it was

4

without going into a small town and a small county in rough country in Texas to get involved, most likely, with corrupt local lawmen. Billy Vail had often said, "Hell, if the local law down there can't straighten the mess out, then the damn people ought to vote in a sheriff that can. This ain't federal business and I ain't wasting deputies on it."

But the day had come when serious business had taken Longarm to Austin and Billy had said, since Longarm was going to be so close, why didn't he go on down to Mason and have a quick look around. However, he had admonished Longarm to give the matter no more attention than it deserved. But there had been complexities to the situation that had intrigued Longarm as a lawman and made him anxious to find out just how deep the corruption ran.

And besides, there was Hannah Diver. She was the sixth youngest of Dalton Diver's ten daughters. People said that old Dalton Diver raised daughters the way other folks raised cattle, for profit, and that he was doing considerably better than most cattlemen. Diver made no attempt to deny or disguise the fact. He was straight-up direct about the way he went about marrying off his daughters. Hannah had been a good example. Before he would let her marry Gus Horne, who was considered, but not proven, to be an outlaw, he had made the man purchase a good, comfortable cabin on deeded land, furnish Hannah with a good milk cow and laying chickens, and provide her with a horse and buggy as well as a saddle horse. In addition he was to give Hannah a vegetable kitchen garden plowed up and planted, put five hundred dollars in the bank in her name, and pay Dalton Diver the sum of one thousand dollars.

Gus Horne had lived up to every commitment, except he'd been called away right after the marriage, leaving Hannah frustrated and disappointed and angry as hell. She had told Longarm that her mother, before she'd died, had talked to her about her wedding night. Hannah had said, "Momma told me that a lady gets deflowered on her wedding night. That her husband comes along and plucks her like a rose. That I'm a bud just waiting to flower and that my husband is going to be the one who makes me open up. Well, I ain't been deflowered and I ain't been plucked and I damn sure ain't opened up! My daddy takes good care of his girls, and I'm gonna send him after that damn Gus Horne if he don't get back here and tend to his business!"

Longarm's correct name was Custis Long, and he had been a deputy United States marshal for a good deal longer than he liked to think about. It seemed that he had been based in Denver, listening to Billy Vail, the chief marshal, tell him where and when he was heading out on another job, for nearly as long as he could remember. He had been shot, he'd been stabbed, he'd nearly been burned to death, he'd nearly died of thirst, of hunger, of bad whiskey, and lack of ammunition. Along the way there had been plenty of women, but there never had been one like Hannah. For one thing, he was pretty sure that she was a virgin and he had never, to use her word, deflowered a virgin. For another, she was married, technically, and Longarm had never knowingly taken another man's wife. But without splitting hairs, he felt that, circumstances being what they were, he would not be acting against his own code of honor if he helped this young lady out—sort of stood in as a surrogate for her missing husband as it were. He had asked himself if he would have been so eager to do the good turn if Hannah were not quite so delectable-looking, but he had avoided answering the question because he didn't think it applied. Hannah already had the body she had, and nothing was going to change the way she looked. Besides, he had told himself, there was an excellent chance that she was going to be a widow before anybody deflowered her. And the woman was curious as hell. She was burning up to know what it was all about, and Longarm had never been one to deny a beautiful woman anything that was within his power to give.

He now said to Deputy Melvin Purliss, "Just hang on a minute. Let me step back inside and tell Mrs. Diver—"

"Horne. She married Gus Horne, you'll recollect."

"Horne then." He stared at Purliss, thinking that what made him the best of Bodenheimer's three deputies was that he was not blood kin of the sheriff. Of the other two, one was a first cousin and the other was a nephew. The relationship showed in both of them. Longarm put his hand on the door latch and said, "You wait here, Purliss. I'll be back right quick."

"You want me to tighten the cinch on yore horse?"

"I don't want you going near my horse. Is that clear? Don't touch any of my stock."

The deputy looked sullen. "You ain't got to be so cranky about it."

Considering what he was about to have to leave behind, Longarm thought that he had full right to be a hell of a lot crankier than he'd shown so far. He said, "Melvin, this better not be another wild-goose chase, or I'm likely to be of a great mind to put you and Bodenheimer and the rest of your bunch in federal prison. How'd you like to spend some time in Kansas, Melvin?"

Purliss backed away, looking down at the ground. He hacked and spat and said sullenly, "Ain't no need take it out on me. I just doin' what I'm told."

"Well, now, I'm telling you to stand right there and don't do nothing. Don't make no noise and don't move out of that spot. Understand?"

Without waiting for an answer, he swung the door open slightly and then slid through and closed it behind him. It was a little after one o'clock on a bright, fall day. Hannah had fixed him a good lunch of stew with meat and vegetables and fresh-baked bread. That, along with a bottle of the Maryland whiskey that he favored and the scent and feel of her, had more than filled him up.

She was still in the bed, lying exactly as he had left her, her light brown head shiny against the white of the pillowcase. He crossed the room and eased down on the side of the bed. Her eyes had been closed, but now they fluttered open. She said, "We gonna do it now?"

The words were more painful than any bullets that had ever pierced his hide. He winced, trying to think of something to say. "Not just this minute, Hannah, darlin'," he said. "I got to run a little errand. But I will be back here tonight."

"Oh, you!" she said angrily. "You ain't no better than the rest." She suddenly flung the covers off her and sat up on the bed. Longarm was suddenly face-to-face with those swelling breasts again. His mouth hungered for the taste of her cherry nipples, and the crotch of his jeans suddenly became too tight. With a swift move he leaned down, turning his head sideways, and took each one of them in turn in his mouth, holding them each a long moment, feeling them going more rigid as he caressed them with his tongue.

Hannah began trembling slightly. She said, "Ooooooooh. Is that part of it?"

Longarm raised his head up. "Yeah," he said huskily.

"I like that," she said, her hazel eyes looking excited. "That feels gooooood."

"Try this," he said. He put his mouth over hers, trying to force it open gently with his tongue. She pulled back until she could see him.

She said, "Are you aimin' to put your tongue in my mouth?"

"Yes," he said, having difficulty controlling his voice. "That's the idea. Then you do with your tongue what you want to."

He leaned in to kiss her again, taking her in his arms.

This time her lips were soft and open and her tongue was a darting, exploring probe. When he finally pulled back she was breathing hard. She said, "I like this. What else can we do?"

He leaned down and kissed the soft mound of her little belly. His breathing was short and hard and there was a pounding in both temples. He straightened up. "Hannah, we can do a whole lot of other things. But we can't right now."

"But you'll come back and show me? I'm willin' to learn."

He swallowed and took a deep breath. "I'm sure you are." He let his breath out in a long sigh. "Hannah, you are about as tasty as pie. I hate like hell to leave you, even for a short time."

"You be back in time for supper? I got a side of beef Daddy brought over in the springhouse. It be of prime age. I'll cut you off a big steak."

Longarm stood up and shook his head regretfully. "I'll be back, Hannah, darlin'. You keep on thinking about how it is gonna be."

"You gonna learn me all about it then?"

"Oh, yes," Longarm said, nodding, his breath getting short again. "I will learn you *all* about it." He leaned down and kissed her. Her tongue came out like a pouncing cat. He started to tell her you saved those kind of kisses for when one of the persons wasn't leaving, but decided not to load the girl up with too much information at one time. He said, glancing at the door, "Otis Bodenheimer had better have *something* up a tree or I'm going to hang him to it."

Her smooth brow furrowed. "Huh?"

"Nothing, Hannah," he said. He patted her on the shoulder and then put on his hat. "I'll be back quick as I can."

But at the door he stopped and turned back. A thought was troubling him, had been troubling him all week. He

9

said, "Hannah, I been meaning to ask you something, but first one thing and then another has been getting in the way." He knew what that one thing was and it didn't have anything to do with law work.

"What?"

He frowned. "Did you know Gus Horne before you married him?"

She shook her head slowly. "No, not really."

"What do you mean by that? Did ya'll court? Did he call on you at your daddy's place? Take you out for carriage rides? Barn dances?"

She looked prim. "Well, Marshal Long, Gus Horne be a outlaw. He couldn't go 'bout like he wanted to. Not here in this county. They laid low mostly, I guess."

He frowned again. "What about after you were married? How was that supposed to work? Was he still going to have to lay low?"

She shrugged. "I don't know. Never thought about it, an' Daddy never said. I reckon you'd have to talk to Daddy about that."

Longarm was still having trouble digesting the situation. Dalton Diver was a well-to-do and respected rancher. He could not understand how he would willingly marry off his daughter to an outlaw. But it seemed impossible to believe that he couldn't have known what Gus Horne was. Longarm said, "Your daddy did know that Gus Horne was a wanted man, didn't he?"

She thought a second, pursing her full lips. "Well, yeah, I reckon. But Daddy said so long as he done his dirty business somewheres else, wasn't none of our affair so long as he behaved at home. I ain't the first one, you know, married into that bunch."

"No, you have a sister that did also. Lives close to here somewhere."

Hannah nodded. "That'd be my sister Sarah. She lives on the next section east, down the river. She married Archie Bowen near a year ago. Course he got kilt." She thought a moment. "You knowed I was the fourth to marry into that gang."

Longarm blinked. He had not "knowed." He said, "No, tell me about it."

Hannah sat up further, causing the blanket to fall down around her hips. Longarm swallowed. It was a sight that it was hard not to be affected by. She said, "First one was my fourth oldest sister, Rebeccah. She married Lester Gaskamp. Little over two years ago it was. Course he was the leader of that bunch when they first commenced their stealin' and whatnot. You know he was killed."

Longarm stood there in some amazement. He'd been in town a full week and this was the first he was hearing about such matters. He said, "No, no, I've never heard the man's name. The one I heard was the leader was Wayne Shaker."

Hannah tossed her head sending her fine, long hair flying in a shimmering sheen of light brown. "Oh, some says he is, some says he ain't. He's a Mason County boy, you know, but he ain't all that bright. They was a lot of hope for Lester, but he got kilt when they was trying to rob a bank in Junction City, and them fool boys didn't know any more about robbing a bank than a mule knows about Santa Claus. They was just startin' out an' ups and tries a big bank like that one in Junction City. That was just plain silly."

"The sister that was married to Lester—Rebeccah?" Hannah nodded.

"Did she get a cabin and land and money?"

"Oh, yes. Boys around here know they might not as well come around unless they got the price of our hand in marriage. Got to be a nice place on a good piece of land. And the land had better be a section, six hundred and forty acres, and the money better be ready to hand. Daddy ain't always so strict about the amount of land as he is about the quality. Now this land on the river

11

ain't nowhere near a section, but Daddy says water is worth a whole bunch of acres of dry land. I don't know if that is so or not, but that is what Daddy says."

Longarm said slowly, "That's three. Any more?"

"Well, yes. I'm kind of ashamed about him so we don't talk about him much. Daddy is the most ashamed of all. Was a boy named Jim Squires. He asked for the hand of my sister Salome, she's my second oldest sister. But he didn't have the price. Well, they was in love and Salome was kicking up a ruckus about the matter, so Daddy said they could go ahead and get hitched, except Salome was goin' to have to live at home until Jim could raise the money for what was needed. When he got that tended to they could live together like man and wife, whatever that is supposed to mean. Well, you wouldn't believe what happened. Jim Squires went off with that bunch and they was going to stick up the mail stage comes down from Austin. Was a little shootin' and that Jim Squires turned tail and run off like a rabbit. We ain't seen hide nor hair of him since. Salome is just plain *mortified*. And I reckon she has got good reason to be. I know I would if a husband of mine pulled some such trick."

Longarm stared at her, dumbfounded. Finally he said, "As a general rule, where do these young men get the kind of money to afford you and your sisters?"

Hannah shrugged. "Steals it, I guess. I don't know. But I know this. They ain't never again none of them goin' to get one of us on credit. Daddy done said that. It's cash on the barrelhead and no exceptions. My word, you ought to have seen Daddy when he got the news about Jim Squires. He just ranted and raved till the world looked level. He's just layin' for that young man to show his face round these parts again. He'll get himself a divorce so quick it'll make his head swim."

"So there have been four of you married into that gang. Any children?"

Hannah gave a hoot of laughter. "Not very likely. Ain't a one of 'em got a chance to do his duty. I ain't the only flower wiltin' on the vine."

Longarm shook his head slowly. "This is about the damnedest situation I reckon I ever run up against. Did your momma give you girls any advice?"

"Advice about what?"

"Well, you don't seem to have any luck with husbands. How did she figure you were supposed to get your petals plucked?"

Hannah said, "She told us all to take the first one came along we took a shine to and get right after it."

"And I'm the first one to come along."

"First one seemed to know what it was all about."

Longarm nodded. "Well, I've got to comment that your daddy has got one of the most unusual businesses going I ever heard of. Seems to be doing right well."

"Oh, yeah. Daddy was always one to find a way to make money."

"Tell me, have all the boys been Mason County boys, all the husbands?"

She shook her head. "Naw. Lester Gaskamp was the only one."

"Where is yours, Gus Horne, from?"

She shook her head. "I don't know. I never passed ten words with the man. When the wedding was over Daddy come up and whispered in his ear and he was gone. Now there is some talk that this Wayne Shaker might be allowed to marry my sister Rebeccah, the one that's been on the vine over two years. Course I hear she ain't been lettin' the ground grow under her feet all that time. Daddy says it would tie things up in a neat package. Daddy don't like no loose strings danglin'. Too many womenfolks around the house to suit Daddy."

"What about the one that married the boy that run off, Squires?"

Hannah pulled her lower lip down. "Why, there's

13

nothin' can be done about that worthless trash till Daddy can arrange to get him kilt. He's just extra baggage right now. Poor Salome can't be free until he shows up, which he ain't going to, or Daddy can find him and set matters straight.''

The knocking came at the door again. Longarm gave it an annoyed look. "Hold up, dammit!" he yelled. He put his hand on the latch. "Hannah, honey, I'll be back just quick as I can. We'll get you deflowered yet.''

"Well, you better," she said.

Longarm nodded, and opened the door and slipped through. He closed it so that Melvin Purliss could not see into the cabin. "This better be kind of important," he said to the deputy.

Chapter 2

Longarm and Deputy Purliss rode through the rough, hilly country, heading west, keeping the brisk little Llano River in sight off to their left. They were pointing toward a place near the Kimble County line some few miles north of the little settlement of Koockville. The country was covered with mesquite, post oak, wild plum, and stunted sycamore and elm. Nothing very big grew on the rocky, craggy hills, not even big trees. But it was rough going. Even at the slow pace Longarm insisted upon, they were constantly dodging and picking their way through the brushy places. It wasn't really bad country, Longarm thought, but it made him think of something a friend of his had once said upon viewing the badlands of Montana. The man had said, "Hell, it's passable. You take something heavy and flatten out all these buttes and rock outcroppings and sharp-pointed hills, and then lay about two foot of topsoil over that, and then cover it with grass—good grass, of course— and add in a bunch of good shade trees and some running water, and turn the sun down about twenty degrees in the summer and up about twenty in the winter, why, you might just have you some pretty decent land." His friend had paused. "Of course, then some sonofabitch

15

is going to go and offer you a bunch of money for it, and you'll take it and get drunk and then, like as not, you'll end up married to a woman will make you more miserable than any land did, and you'd do anything if you could only have the old badlands back and give up the wife and the money. So all in all, I reckon we better leave the country like it is, because I ain't never got drunk or married I wasn't sorry about it later.''

He wondered what that friend of his would make of Hannah Diver and Gus Horne, not to mention Dalton Diver and his crop of daughters. It appeared to Longarm that Diver had hit on the best scheme for making money since a horse trader taught his stock to ''home'' every time they got loose. That trader had sold a hundred horses, and still had the five he'd come with when he quit the country. To Longarm it appeared that Dalton Diver was doing the same thing, the way his daughters were becoming widows. Four married women and the bulk of them still virgins. He reckoned that was a part of the situation he was going to have to dig deeper in.

But maybe it was all for naught. Perhaps Sheriff Bodenheimer really did have the gang trapped in a cave along the river. Longarm doubted it, but it might be so. And if that was the case, he was just going to have time to deflower Hannah before heading back to Denver and new duties.

At Purliss's direction, they left the hilly part of the country and headed down toward the river. There they turned west again and rode along beside the little stream. As they rounded a bend, a line of sheer bluffs rose up on the far side of the river. The bluffs were perhaps fifty feet high in some places, and so steep they could only be climbed or traversed by a few outcroppings or ridges that provided scanty footpaths along the faces. Here and there Longarm could see holes in the face of the bluffs, and he supposed it must be one such that Bodenheimer was talking about. They were riding along a little strip of sand that ran beside the river and separated the water from the brush line. Still, the sand was so cluttered with stray stones and rocks that a man had to be careful of his horse, hold the pace down, and keep an eye on the ground. He was riding a horse he'd bought in Austin, a horse that had taken his eye. The animal was a deep-chested bay with long clean lines and a strong, if long, neck. The whole package added up to quick speed when you needed it, with sure signs of endurance in the long lean muscles and the iron-hard condition of the mount. As a deputy U.S. marshal, Longarm could requisition horses from any federal government installation that had them. But he was almost as much a horse trader as he was a whiskey drinker, and almost as much a whiskey drinker as he was a poker player, and almost as much a poker player as he was a man who admired and appreciated good-looking women. As a consequence he made it a habit, when he was in good horse country, to trade for likely animals, have them shipped to Denver at government expense, and then make a profit off their resale. His boss, Billy Vail, had several times expressed grave doubts about the legality, much less the morality, of such a practice. Longarm had replied that, considering what the government paid him in salary, it was the only way he could afford to go on being a deputy marshal without starving to death. But Billy Vail had said, "If you'd go ahead and take the promotion to chief marshal, you wouldn't be one jump ahead of the poorhouse. Ain't nothin' but yore own stubbornness keepin' you from it."

Longarm had said with a laugh, "Billy, I'd have to be like you. I swear, I can't bring myself to sit behind a desk all day. I'll just have to keep on like I been going. But I like my job, Billy. Honest to Pete I do. Why, if somebody was to give me a hundred thousand dollars, I'd just go on being a deputy marshal until it had all run out."

Longarm glanced over at the river now as he rode. It

was about fifty or sixty yards wide and about two to four feet deep. Where it ran into rocks or a sharp down-grade, it roared and spewed foam and turned into white-water rapids. Longarm thought the clear stream was just as pretty as a good many little rivers in Colorado. The Llano, he knew, started from spring-fed streams about eighty miles away. It ran forty miles to the town of Llano, and then on to Burnett, where it emptied into the Colorado River, a much bigger river that was headed for the Gulf of Mexico on the coast in Matagorda County.

He said to Purliss, "How much further?"

"Pretty quick, Marshal." Purliss pointed ahead. "We go round that little spit of land sticking out up yonder an' they ought to be in sight."

The spit was guarded by a growth of thorny hackberry trees, and Longarm was forced to swing his horse out into the edge of the stream, splashing water, to get around the obstacle. When he'd pulled his mount back up onto the sandy strip, he could see several horsemen ahead sitting their animals and looking at Longarm and Purliss. After a hundred yards he could see the black, longcoat-covered figure of Otis Bodenheimer setting himself apart from the other men.

The deputy said, "Thar' they be, Marshal."

"I'd of never knowed if you hadn't told me, Purliss." He gave the deputy a look. "Melvin, this is the only county in any state or territory I ever been in where they'd actually give a man like you a gun and a badge."

The little deputy looked at him, startled, trying to see if Longarm was joshing him. "Well, Marshal, I don't—"

"Shut up, Purliss," Longarm said. "I ain't in no mood to listen to you talk." Longarm was thinking of Hannah back in the cabin. If Purliss had waited another hour Longarm would now be a very satisfied man.

Then they were coming up on the small party. Long-arm counted seven men besides Bodenheimer. His other

18

two deputies were there. The nephew was Claude Botts; the cousin was Earl Bodenheimer. As near as Longarm could tell, there wasn't an ounce of brains on either side to choose from. If you threw Purliss in, the content might rise a little, but not much.

He pulled his horse up as the party started walking their horses toward him, the sheriff in the lead. Bodenheimer gave him a stiff little nod and said, "Well, you've taken yore time gettin' here, Marshal, but I reckon it be just as well. They ain't done no stirrin' round."

Longarm looked at the fat man's fat face with distaste. "To begin with, *Otis* . . ." He managed to say the sheriff's name so that it sounded like a bad odor. "To begin with, I don't know what in hell you are sending for me for. Ain't you the damn sheriff? Or is that just an ugly rumor floating around that I hope isn't true."

But there was no insulting the man. He sat his horse, giving Longarm a placid look. "I tol' Melvin there to 'splain to you that parts of this river is in dispute between us and Kimble County and I don't want to have no disputes with Sheriff Estes over crowdin' in on his territory."

Longarm said patiently, "Dammit, Otis, I have told you a half a dozen times you can cross county lines when you are in hot pursuit."

Bodenheimer had a cud of tobacco in his jaw. He sat chewing it like a cow, his moon face innocent of any sign of understanding. "Ain't no way to say for shore 'bout a thing like that. Sher'ff Estes is kinda edgy 'bout matters here lately. Don't want to go rilin' him. Thought it would be as easy to have you out."

Longarm gave him a disgusted look. "Yeah, I imagine Sheriff Estes is a little edgy at you, but it ain't got a damn thing to do with hot pursuit or crossing into his county. I would imagine he's getting damn tired of you making a home for a gang of robbers who are stealing in his towns and then running back here to hide. And as for it being just as easy to send for me . . ." Longarm rose in his stirrups a little and reached out and jabbed Bodenheimer hard on the breastbone with a thick forefinger. "Next time I recommend you give it some more thought before you just up and send for me. I might otherwise be occupied."

Bodenheimer pulled back from the piledriving forefinger, but otherwise gave no sign he understood that he was being reprimanded. He said, "Tryin' to do the smart thang, Marshal."

Longarm made a disgusted sound. The first day he'd arrived in Mason County he'd decided that Otis Bodenheimer was dangerous—to the citizens of Mason County. His opinion had only gone downhill from there. He said, "Smart? Bodenheimer, you'd have to improve to just be dangerously dumb. All right, what have you got here?"

Bodenheimer straightened in his saddle, and pointed across the river toward the face of the bluff. "You see the mouth of that cave over yonder? Well, we got pretty good reason to reckon that bunch is holed up in there."

Longarm turned slightly in his saddle to look across the river. About halfway up the bluff face he could see a hole about five feet in diameter. It could be a cave or nothing more than a dimple in the cliff face. Longarm judged it to be no more than eighty or ninety yards away from where they were standing. He could see a little ledge that ran below the opening and then made a ragged trip to the top of the cliff. He studied it a moment and then said wonderingly, "What makes you think they are in there, Bodenheimer? Or do you just *hope* they are there?"

The sheriff spat tobacco juice and then turned in his saddle to locate a face among the silent men around him. He said, pointing, "Elton Miles thar', he seen 'em. Ain't that right, Elton?"

Elton Miles was an ordinary-looking little man with a growth of whiskers and a mustache stained with tobacco juice. He nodded vigorously. "Yessir, yessir, that be right, Shur'ff. I seen 'em. 'Bout 'leven o'clock it was this mornin'. Seen the bunch of 'em riding through them thickets over yonder. Musta been five, six, seven of 'em. I wasn't too anxious to be callin' no attention to myself, so I hung pleny far back. But it was the bunch. I'd swear it."

Longarm studied the man for a moment and said, "You mean you saw five or six men. Is that right?"

Elton Miles bobbed his head. "Yessir, yessir. Shore did. Make no mistake."

"You see them go in the cave?"

Elton Miles opened his mouth to say something, and then thought better of it and closed it. He opened it again and said, "Well, not prezactly."

"What do you mean, not prezactly?"

Elton Miles looked uncomfortable. "Like I wuz tellin' them, Marshal, I kinda hung back in that wild plum thicket. I didn't want them boys gettin' after me. But I seen 'em headin' fer the river, an' then it seem like I heered their horses in the water. Little while after that I kind of snuck around where I could see the river. Got off my horse an' went to sneakin' round and they was gone. Wasn't no sign of 'em, hide or hair."

Longarm looked across the river at the cliff face. There were several ravines cutting through it where one could leave the riverbed and make the ground on the other side. To get to the cave a horseman would have to climb the ravine to the high ground and then turn his horse loose, and after that, make his way down the precarious little ledge to the mouth of the cave. And Elton Miles hadn't seen anything. Apparently he hadn't seen where they had crossed or where they had gone once they had cleared the river. But to be sure, Longarm asked the little man again.

Elton Miles blinked. "Seen 'em go in the cave? Why, nosir, nosir. I went and tol' the shur'ff what I seen and he got him a bunch together and we figured out they was a-hidin' in that cave."

It was a Saturday afternoon, a crisp cool fall day at its best. And, Longarm thought, he was standing here with seven of the dumbest sonofabitches he'd ever met when, by rights, he should be in a bed in a cabin with a young lady by the name of Hannah.

He let his eyes rove over the bunch with Bodenheimer. *"Otis,"* he said, "I know that three of these men are your deputies. Who are the other damn fools?"

Bodenheimer didn't blink. He said stoutly, "They be good citizens that I deputized. I didn't know what to expect. Could have been in a gunfight."

Longarm looked at the men and shook his head. "Bodenheimer, you are likely to bankrupt the saloons you keep taking such good citizens out of town. Now, what have you done to see if, by whatever wild chance, the outlaw gang might be over there?"

Bodenheimer chewed his cud of tobacco. "Been waitin' on you, Marshal."

"Where are their horses? Didn't you send anybody across the river to get on top to see if their horses might be tied there? You didn't really think they could lead their horses down that ledge and into that cave, did you?" He said it, hoping that Bodenheimer would have some idea of what he was talking about.

"Well, Marshal, I didn't reckon we ought to cross over. Might be in Kimble County."

Longarm shook his head. "Well, did you at least fire a few shots into the cave to see if you got a reaction?"

The sheriff thought a moment, and then he looked around at the two deputies that had stayed with him. They stared blankly back. He said, "Well, no. Now that you mention it."

"Why not?"

The sheriff looked at the cave. "Weeell, I reckon we didn't think of it. Besides, I ain't all that sure what Elton seen. He never tracked them to the river. Was a good quarter mile back yonder." He motioned over his shoulder. "Where he spotted 'em. Ain't no tellin' who might be in that cave."

Longarm snorted. "Might be a voter, Sheriff. You're a man ought not to kill off anybody would vote for you." Without taking his eyes off the sheriff's face Longarm pulled his rifle out of the boot. He levered a shell into the chamber and swiveled in the saddle, putting the rifle to his shoulder as he did. He aimed at the top lip of the cave, making sure that the bullets would bury themselves into the clay roof. He cocked the hammer and fired. The rifle boomed and echoed in the canyon created by the river. Nothing happened. He levered home another cartridge and fired again. Still nothing moved. In quick succession he got off two more shots and then lowered his rifle. A half minute passed and then a sow coon, followed by four half-grown ones, came boiling out of the cave and went racing up the little ledge. They disappeared over the top. Longarm laughed. He reached into his shirt pocket, where he carried his spare ammunition, and slowly reloaded his rifle. "Well, Elton Miles was right about one thing," he said. "There was five of them." He gave the bunch a disgusted look. "Did you know, Sheriff, that it is a felony crime to waste the time of a federal marshal? I've about half a mind to jail the lot of you on that one count."

The horsemen shifted about, looking at each other uneasily. Sheriff Bodenheimer said, "I reckon I never heered of any such law. But ain't nobody set out to waste federal government time. I done what I figured to be right."

"Yeah?" Longarm let his eyes rove over the men. He was conscious of Purliss letting his horse stray away from near Longarm. The marshal looked at Elton Miles.

He said, "Elton, did you really see a group of horsemen? Did you see anybody cross the river? What did you see?"

The little man opened his mouth and then shut it. He opened it again, but nothing came out. Finally he made a sound like a squeak and said, "Marshal, I'm pretty shore I seed som'thin'. I ain't together shore what it was, but the shur'ff here thought we better get on out here an' have us a good look around. The shur'ff has ast us all to be on the lookout for any strange business round about. I done what he ast. Looked queer to me, bunch ridin' round in here."

Longarm stared at him. "What is today, Elton? What is today in Mason?"

The little man blinked. "Why, why it's Satt'day. Yessir, Satt'day."

"First Saturday of the month."

"Yessir."

"And what do they do on the first Saturday of the month?" He didn't wait for an answer. He said, "It's Trades Day, Elton. Or didn't you notice. I'm a stranger here, but when I walked out of my hotel room I knew it was Trades Day. Square was already full of folks bringing in various items and loose livestock to trade."

Elton Miles looked down at the ground.

"You sure you didn't see a couple of hombres bringing in a few head of horses to swap?" Longarm asked him.

Elton Miles kept his eyes on the ground. "Marshal, I ain't right shore. All's I knows is the shur'ff set pretty good store by it."

Longarm switched his eyes to Bodenheimer. "Well, *Otis*? What do *you* reckon?"

The sheriff shifted in his stirrups. "Wa'l, I done what I thought best."

"Bullshit," Longarm said in disgust. "You wouldn't know best if you had it embroidered across your vest.

You better get on back to town and quit wearing your horses out."

Longarm would have liked nothing better than to have turned back around and ridden straight back to Hannah's cabin. But she had a reputation to maintain and, even if she was in an unconsummated marriage with an outlaw, she had to keep up appearances. Longarm felt he had no choice but to ride back to town with the group that had come to flush the outlaws out of the cave. The sheriff's "posse," he thought with disgust. He'd interrupted what had promised to be a memorable afternoon to waste it on such a fool's errand. His only hope was to get back to town, let himself be seen, and then slip away and head back for Hannah's. This time, however, he wouldn't let anyone, especially in the sheriff's office, know where he was going.

They rode out of the woods and picked up the Brady road about a mile southwest of town. Longarm rode out ahead of the group, not caring for their company in the slightest. Looking up at the sun, he calculated it to be about four in the afternoon. He had a watch in his pants pocket, but it was easier to glance at the sky. He knew he wouldn't be off more than a quarter of an hour.

As they rounded a bend, Longarm saw a man riding toward them on the road from town. He was galloping his horse and waving his free hand. Longarm could see his mouth moving, but he couldn't hear the man's words. He pulled up his horse and stopped, content to let the man come to him. The rest of the group stopped behind Longarm. He sat his horse, resting his hands on the pommel of his saddle. When the man was about a hundred yards away Longarm could hear him yelling for the sheriff. Longarm turned in his saddle and glanced back at Bodenheimer. "He wants you, Sheriff. I'd figure that makes him a runaway madman."

Bodenheimer didn't respond. Longarm looked at him

and shook his head. He had hoped to insult the sheriff so much he'd try to retaliate, and then Longarm would have him removed from office one way or another. But the man wouldn't rise to the bait. He simply took Longarm's jabs like the lump of unleavened dough he was.

Then the man on the road was pulling his horse up to a jolting, skidding stop. Longarm didn't know the man, but he clearly understood the words the man was yelling at Bodenheimer. He said, "Sheriff, they done robbed the auction barn! Stole all the damn money!"

Longarm turned and looked at Bodenheimer. All the sheriff did was blink, but Longarm's look was grim. If he was going to be played for a fool, he wanted it to be by someone who was at least smarter than a milk cow, which was what Bodenheimer reminded him of.

The auction barn was located seven miles on the other side of town, on the Llano road almost at the Llano County line. It had been deliberately located there so it could draw trade from as big an area as possible. It was a major cattle and horse trading market. A man might take an individual horse or cow or a few goats into the town square on market day, or Trades Day, but the auction barn dealt in volume and attracted cattlemen and horse ranchers from a considerable area. The barn usually held its bigger auctions on Trades Days so as to take advantage of the number of out-of-country people who would be coming to the area.

It took them an hour and a half to ride through the town of Mason and then cover the seven miles to the auction barn. Longarm had expected most of the traders would have gone home. The robbery, as best Longarm could figure out from the excited man who'd brought the news, had taken place some four hours previously. It was pushing six o'clock and sundown by the time Longarm rode up to the barn. He estimated there were still forty to fifty men standing around, looking agitated.

They started yelling as soon as they saw Bodenheimer. Longarm left the sheriff to deal with the crowd while he dismounted and went into the cashier's office by the outside door. It was in that office that the robbery had taken place. The cashier was a middle-aged lady, the wife of the auction barn owner, John Ownsby. There were several other people in the office, but Longarm cleared them all out except for Ownsby and his wife. The owner was having a glass of whiskey and his wife was drinking coffee. Both, Longarm could tell, were considerably shaken by what had happened. Longarm sat down and accepted a whiskey from Ownsby. Mrs. Ownsby was seated at her desk, while her husband leaned against the wall and nursed his drink. He said, looking worried, "Marshal, I don't know what in hell to do." He gestured outside the building. "I got a lot of men out there who have bought and paid for a bunch of animals, paid cash, and I can't let them take their own property away because there ain't no money to pay the men who owned the stock that they bought." He ran his hand over his face. He was a man pushing fifty, and his hair was streaked with gray. He went on. "It's one hell of a mess. And where was that damn Bodenheimer and his deputies when we got held up? Hell, clean over on the other side of the damn county. And that sonofabitch knows we deal in considerable cash here."

"Does he ever send deputies around?" Longarm asked, curious. "Or come around himself?"

Ownsby looked disgusted. "Hell, no. The sonofabitch said they wasn't nobody going to go to a place where they was half a hundred able-bodied men and hold it up." Ownsby leaned forward. "Well, they never come in no place where they was half a hundred able-bodied men." He gestured around the small office. "They come in here, where the money was, and where they wasn't nothin' but a nice little lady to scare the hell out of!"

Mrs. Ownsby put her hand to her breast and looked

toward the ceiling while she took a deep breath. She said, "Marshal, John and I got caught in a flood in a wagon that drowned the team in its traces, and I wasn't nowhere near as scared as I was when them two men come in here waving guns around and demanding the money. Heavens, they didn't have to demand it." She gestured at the top of her desk. "It was all right here. All they had to do was lean down and pick it up."

"How much was taken?" Longarm asked.

Before anyone could answer, the door opened from the outside and Otis Bodenheimer started in. Longarm wheeled in his chair. "Stay outside, Bodenheimer."

The sheriff protested. "Hell, Marshal, this is my business. This done taken place in my county."

"Couldn't have happened nowhere else. So we agree about that. But I don't want you in here. You get outside and tend to the electorate, especially men who have got money or stock coming. See if you can explain what happened to them."

But Bodenheimer stood his ground. "I'm the sheriff here," he said stoutly. "And this is my affair to handle. This is my business."

Longarm stood up. "Bodenheimer, if you don't get out of here I'm going to have to give Mister Ownsby an announcement to make to the crowd."

Bodenheimer frowned. "What's that?"

"I said I'd have to whisper a few words into Mister Ownsby's ear that he could announce to the crowd."

Bodenheimer was still frowning. "What, uh, kind of announcement?"

"That's just the thing," Longarm said. "You won't know until it's too late."

Bodenheimer looked uncertain. "I ain't right sure I'm following you."

"What I'm saying, Bodenheimer, is once Ownsby tells the crowd what I got in mind, you'll be running for your life."

The sheriff took a step backward. "Now, hold on," he said. "You better not go to spreadin' no tales about me."

"It won't be a tale," Longarm said. "Now, are you going to get out of here or do I send out Mister Ownsby?"

The sheriff looked back and forth from Longarm to Ownsby. "Why, why, you are threatening me with what I don't know. That ain't fair. I ain't got no way of knowing what you might have Mister Ownsby say to that bunch. They be pretty upset, Marshal. Ain't no time for rash doings."

"Then I reckon you better get the hell out of here and talk to them yourself. That way you can control the situation."

Bodenheimer blinked and felt behind him for the door handle. "Well, all right, Marshal, but you and I is got to have a little talk. We both on the same side."

"Right now I want you on the other side of that door. That's the only side I want you to be on. The other."

"I'm goin' then. Damned if I know what this is all about."

Longarm watched, without a word, until Bodenheimer had let himself out and closed the door. Then he turned and sat back down in the chair. "Now then," he said, "how much did they get?"

But Ownsby was staring at Longarm. "What was that all about?"

Longarm shrugged. "Nothing."

"First time I ever seen one lawman run off another one from the site of a theft. Strikes me as passing strange."

"Maybe that's because federal officers don't do business the way you are used to your sheriff doing."

Ownsby gave a snort. "That's for damn shore. Any change in that direction would be a relief."

Longarm said, "Now then, Mrs. Ownsby, can you tell me how much was taken?"

She fluttered her hands. "Well, I can't say to the dollar, not until I get all of the sales receipts in from the man what runs the auction, the auctioneer."

Ownsby said, "It was all the morning receipts. Them as had done their business and come in and paid Vera." He nodded his head at his wife. "Mrs. Ownsby. Whatever that figure come out to be. It will be a good piece of change."

"More than, say, two thousand dollars?"

"Oh, good heavens, yes. Day like today, brisk as it was, it would be closer on to four thousand than two."

Longarm shook his head slowly. "That's a bunch of money to expect to find sitting out here in a grove of mesquite trees. Is it pretty common knowledge that ya'll handle such funds out here?"

Ownsby pulled a face. "I wouldn't say every Tom, Dick, or Harry knowed about it, but it wasn't no secret. You come out here and stand around awhile and see a pen of horses go through and fetch a thousand dollars, and you see a man pay for them in cash, you'd kind of get the idea that we had some money behind the counter."

"Yes, but doesn't the man that sold the horses step up and take it right away?"

Ownsby shook his head. "Naw. Don't work that way. First we got to remove our commission, and then we pay the seller by check. But it don't happen one, two, three. Once the buyer has paid for his stock he goes around to inspect them. That all takes time. We don't okay the sale until buyer and seller is satisfied. That's what makes a auction barn different than trading out of a wagon on the town square. You never know what you'll be getting there, but we guarantee the swap. And if the buyer pays by check, it's us as stands to lose if his check ain't no good. And that can hold up a trade.

30

On some big checks with a buyer that ain't from this part of the country or ain't got no standing with us, why, we'll hold up the trade until we can wire about the man's check. And if a seller wants to be paid in cash, we will try and accommodate him.''

"They come around one o'clock. Wouldn't they have gotten more money if they'd held up until, say, five?"

Ownsby shook his head. "Not necessarily. We shut down at about one, and don't crank up again until three. By five o'clock, we might have paid off a lot of our sellers in cash and might have less money than at one o'clock.''

Longarm looked at Mrs. Ownsby. "Ma'am, I take it you were in here by yourself when the robbers called?"

She fluttered her hands in the air. "Oh, my stars, yes! My heart like to have stopped when they come through that door with them big guns in their hands.''

"How many were there?"

"They was only two come in here, but I could see they was about four more right outside the door.'' She pointed at a little window beside the door. Longarm looked over his shoulder. He could see Bodenheimer and his deputies talking to a group of men. She said, "They was sitting their horses right by the door. One of them was holding the horses of the two who was in here a-robbin' me.''

"How'd you know the men outside were robbers?"

"They was wearing bandannas 'cross their faces just like the ones come in here, wasn't they.''

"So the men that came in here had their faces covered?"

"Well, up to their eyes. And they had their hats pulled low.''

"So you don't have any idea who they were? Or if you'd ever seen them before.''

Ownsby said, "Mother, didn't you say one of them walked kind of familiar?''

31

She frowned. "Now, Marshal, I ain't sure enough about this to swear by it, but the shorter one of the two come in here kind of had a hitch in his get-along. I've seen it before, in town, but I can't put a name or a face to the walk."

"Nothing else?"

Ownsby said, "She told me right after it happened that the leader, I reckon that would be Wayne Shaker, was riding a paint horse."

Longarm shook his head in disbelief. He had heard several times that the leader of the gang rode a paint horse, but he could not bring himself to believe it. It was common coin that a paint horse had to be bred back to his own line so many times to get the variety of colors in his coat that all the quality was bred out of the animal so far as making a good mount. Longarm had never known of a paint horse that had much endurance or staying power, and if there was anything an outlaw required in a mount it was staying power. A robber had to have the means to get clear of a robbery and then put some distance between himself and the men that would be coming after him. And he couldn't do that on a paint, at least not any paint that Longarm had ever come upon. He said, "That's the damnedest thing I ever heard of. Mister Ownsby, you ever heard of a man that needs to make some tracks riding a paint horse?"

Ownsby shook his head. "Not me. And that's why most folks that know anything are of the mind that that gang holds around here close. I don't understand why that damn Otis Bodenheimer can't flush them out. Hell, this is one of the smallest counties around. Fat as he is, looks like he'd stumble over them."

"Have you ever seen Wayne Shaker, Mister Ownsby?"

The man shook his head. "Naw. I never even heard of him until a year ago. But everybody says he's a Mason County boy. Beats the hell out of me why. I can't find nobody that knowed his folks or him or anything about him." He shook his head. "Beats the liver out of me."

Longarm asked a few more questions of the couple, and then told them that he would do everything he could to see that the money was recovered but that he wasn't too hopeful. Ownsby said, "Marshal, I don't know what to do about this mess. It's got me wringing my hands. It wasn't our money as was taken, but we was keeping it for the folks what had it coming. If we have to make good on such a sum, I reckon it will come close to breaking us." He shook his head. "It was a mean piece of luck, Marshal. If I'd been in here maybe I could've sung out or something, alerted the crowd. They'd have made short work of that half a dozen crooks and no mistake. But Mother here, like any women, was scared to death. She wanted them to get on away from her and quit waving those guns."

Longarm recommended that Ownsby not pay out any money for at least forty-eight hours. He said, "I don't see where the law says you owe the money so far as that goes."

Ownsby said, "Oh, that don't make no difference. I run a honest business here, Marshal. I'll go broke before I'll lose the trust of my neighbors and customers."

"Just hold up on breaking yourself. Let me see what I can do."

An hour and a half later Longarm was riding into Mason with Bodenheimer, his three deputies, and Elton Miles. The men that Bodenhiemer had deputized to go to the river with him had disappeared.

Longarm paid no attention to the men riding with him. He headed his horse straight to the sheriff's office, dismounted, and went in without a look back. Once inside, he sat down at Boenheimer's desk and then turned in the swivel chair to face the door. The men came in one at a time, with Elton Miles the last to enter. Bodenheimer stared uncertainly at Longarm sitting behind his desk. "Uh, Marshall," he said, "I reckon you are in my seat."

Longarm ignored the remark. "Sheriff, you and your two blood-kin relatives are under arrest. Purliss, for the time being you are not. Bodenheimer, I want you and those other two idiots with you to very carefully unbuckle your gunbelts and lay them on this desk. And it is my advice that you be real careful how you do it. Don't make me nervous, or else I might draw my weapon and start making a hell of a lot of noise in here."

Bodenheimer stared at him. He said, "Huh?"

Chapter 3

Longarm said, "Huh, hell. Pay attention. You and those two deputies of yours are under arrest. Now get them damn gunbelts on this desk. Quick and careful."

Bodenheimer took a step backward. He was at the front of the line of men who had come in the door. His cousin and his nephew turned and looked at him, uncertainty on their faces. Bodenheimer said, "You can't arrest me. I'm the sheriff. This is my county."

Longarm sat up straight. "Don't make me get up from this chair, Bodenheimer. If I go to the trouble of getting up, I'm going to feel obliged to do something. Am I making myself clear to you, *Sheriff*?"

Bodenheimer said, a little whine in his voice, "You ain't got the right to do this, Marshal. You lock me up in my own county and you've ruined me."

Longarm said grimly, "Better I lock you up than the people of this county string you up."

"Whatever in the world are you talkin' about?"

"Listen, *Otis* . . . You been getting away with murder for several years because that bunch of cutthroats you've been harboring within the confines of Mason County have done all their robbing in other places. But now they have put you in a pretty fix by robbing the auction barn.

They didn't rob Mister Ownsby and his wife. They robbed the folks that have been dumb enough to vote for you. Maybe you are so damned ignorant you couldn't see how riled up that crowd was. They blame you, Bodenheimer. And as soon as they find out you were on the other side of the county on a wild-goose chase and that you lured me out there, they are going to be fit to be tied. Except that ain't what I think they'll do with the rope.'' Longarm stood up, though he did not draw his revolver. All five of the men standing there took an instinctive step backward. Longarm went on.

"You're a crook, Bodenheimer. There's two things that smell awful when they go bad and dead fish is one of them. The other one is crooked law. I can't stand the smell of either one. So I am going to put you in a jail cell until I get this mess straightened out. Now put your damn gunbelts on the top of this desk. *Now!*''

They all jumped back, but then, with Bodenheimer in the lead, one by one they deposited their weapons on the desk. Melvin Purliss, who hadn't understood, had to be stopped by Longarm from doing the same thing. "No, Melvin," Longarm said. "I said just Bodenheimer and his kinfolks. And not you either, Elton Miles. I don't think you did anything wrong. I think the sheriff put it into your head to report what you hadn't seen. You can get out of here now."

When Elton Miles had left, Longarm said to Deputy Purliss, "Melvin, I am promoting you to jailer."

The little deputy frowned. "What?"

"You are going to be the jailer over these three prisoners here." Longarm gestured at Bodenheimer and his kinfolks. "I don't want you out on the street doing anything. Your job is to stay in this jail and keep these men behind bars. See that they get fed and watered, but don't let them out for any reason. And you better not let them escape, Melvin."

Deputy Purliss was still looking uncertain, his gaze

shifting back and forth from Longarm to the frowning face of Sheriff Bodenheimer. He said, "I don't know about this, Marshal."

"Well, I do," Longarm said. "And I want to acquaint you with a little bit of federal law. If you let federal prisoners escape, which these are, then you have to serve their time in their place. Now I figure these boys are going to get about twenty-five years apiece for what I'm going to charge them with. You let them escape and I won't go to hunting them down, I'll come after you. And three times twenty-five is seventy-five years. Keep that in mind, Melvin, when you think about getting careless. Now put them in their cells."

Before they could move, Bodenheimer said, his voice trembling, "Marshal, we ain't done no wrong. And you can't prove we did."

Longarm stared at him for a long moment. Finally he said, "Otis, now you have taken to insulting my intelligence. To begin with, you've had a bandit operating around here for a couple of years who rode a damn *paint* horse. Otis, *nobody* rides a paint that has very far to go or has to go very fast. If you can't catch a bandit riding a paint horse, then you ought not to be in office. And then you had the gall to call me out on that wild-goose chase to the other side of the county. You must think I am a damn fool. Otis, if you are not directly involved with that gang, then you are dumber than I think you are, and that is pretty damn dumb indeed. I hope they have made it worth your while, because you and your cousin and your nephew are going to spend a lot of time in Kansas, and not the prettiest part of the state either. Now get the hell back in those cells before I consider that you are all three trying to escape and have to shoot you in the attempt!"

He sat down at the sheriff's desk and put his boots up while Purliss, reluctantly and timidly, escorted the three men back to cells behind the office. Longarm could hear doors clanging and keys jangling and a few curses. He was frankly amazed that no one had called out Bodenheimer before. Surely all the people in the county couldn't be so dumb as not to see that they weren't exactly getting their money's worth from the sheriff.

Of course Longarm was of the opinion that the situation went a good deal deeper than just the sheriff. He didn't know how he was going to go about digging into the heart of the matter, but it had to be done. Though it could only be done if the good citizens of Mason County wanted it done, and he wasn't so sure they did. He had a feeling that most everyone in the county knew what was going on and approved. Mason was a poor county, and had damn little industry or commerce. Goat raising was about the only moneymaker. That and fugitive harboring, he told himself. It might well be that making a hideout for a gang of bandits was such an important part of the economy that public opinion would be against jailing the members of the gang. He didn't, for the moment, quite know how he was going to handle that part. But he had a pretty good idea that the robbery at the auction barn might have changed public opinion in a big way. Now the outlaws had gone to stealing local money. That was a horse of a different color—and in this case, a horse of many different colors. He sat there in the chair, listening to Purliss completing his task, and admitted to himself that he wouldn't have bothered locking the sheriff up before. No jury would convict him, and he would be back outside damn near before you could roll and smoke a cigarette. But the robbery of the auction house had changed all that. He doubted that Bodenheimer would be very popular, even with his own kin.

Melvin Purliss came back into the office, shutting the iron-bound door that led back to the cells behind him. He hung the big ring of keys up carefully, and then stood uncertainly looking at Longarm.

Longarm glanced up at him. "What?"

Purliss shifted from one foot to the other. "Marshal, I ain't right shore I feel right about this. I ain't never heered of arresting the sheriff before."

Longarm waved a hand at him. "Done all the time, Melvin. All the time. I'd hate to count all the sheriffs I've arrested in my time. Otis ain't the first crooked one I come across. But this time it might be for his own good. When word gets around that a lot of citizens lost money out there at the auction barn, they are going to come looking for Bodenheimer. He might be well off inside a jail cell. Hard to hang a man in there. Ceiling ain't high enough."

Purliss took his hat off and scratched at his hair. "You reckon the shur'ff knowed about that robbery in advance?"

Longarm gave Purliss a slanted look. He brought his feet to the floor and stood up. "Yeah, I think Bodenheimer knew about the robbery." He reached out a blunt forefinger and touched the deputy in the chest. "I ain't all that sure, Melvin, that you didn't know about it."

Purliss opened his mouth, looking a little pale at Longarm's sudden announcement. He said, stuttering slightly, "Tha-tha-that ain't true, Marshal. I ain't never knowed nothin'. I am completely ignorant!"

Longarm laughed. "If you say so, Melvin." He started toward the door, then stopped and looked back. "I'll probably know before you do whether you need me or not, but if you do, I'm going to stay in town tonight. I'll either be at the hotel or the Elite Saloon playing poker."

"What'll I do while I go home fer supper?"

Longarm was about to open the front door of the jail. He looked back. "Oh, you can't go home to supper, Melvin. In fact you can't leave this jailhouse."

Melvin's mouth fell open. "Wha-what-what am I supposed to do. I mean my wife ain't—"

"I'll get them to send you supper over from the hotel

dining room. That reminds me. I need to tell them they got three more prisoners to feed.''

''But-but, Marshal. My wife. I can't stay up here all night!''

Longarm gave him a grave look. ''Melvin, if they come in the middle of the night, some mob with a lynch rope, you got to be here to stop them until I can come over and help you. No, Deputy, you are in to stay.''

He walked out the door, shutting it behind him, leaving the deputy staring after him, his mouth open. As Longarm stepped across the dusty street to the hotel on the other side of the courthouse square, he thought, ''Take that, you little sonofabitch. I bet you'll give it some thought before you go to busting in on me at the wrong time again.''

The thought of Hannah made him pause in mid-stride and look in the direction of the river. It wasn't but a couple of miles to her cabin, and he didn't reckon it was much past eight o'clock. And he had told her he'd be back that evening and she'd cook supper. He'd deliberately left his horse in front of the sheriff's office on the chance he might need the animal later. He'd planned to eat supper at the hotel and then move his horse over to the front of the Elite Saloon. If things were still quiet later on he would take the horse to the livery stable.

So all he had to do was retrace his steps to the front of the jail and mount up, and twenty minutes later he'd be at Hannah's cabin. But it didn't feel right. There could be trouble in town over Bodenheimer, either because he'd been arrested or because he hadn't been hung. Longarm couldn't very well leave Melvin Purliss to face such a situation. No, the best idea was to see what transpired during the night. He could go out to Hannah's sometime the next morning. Anyway, the older he got, the more of a morning man he was becoming. He shrugged and continued on across the lawn of the courthouse with the big, stone, two-story building rising up to his left. It was a mighty imposing edifice, a little overbuilt for a county such as Mason that didn't have that much courthouse business. But Longarm figured the contractor who'd built the courthouse was a member of one of the big families, and he'd been able to milk it for all it was worth. So he had just kept constructing and constructing and constructing.

Longarm went into the hotel and got his key. He had a front room on the ground floor with a bed that was less lumpy than most he'd slept in. But what distinguished Mason's sole hotel was its dining room. The food was surprisingly good, and Longarm went directly there, having washed his face and hands. He could have used a shave and he could have used a bath, but he didn't have a needful feeling for either. He'd get slicked up before he went out to Hannah's the next day. What he mainly wanted to do was to get some supper eaten and then get over to the Elite Saloon and see if a certain gent was sitting in at the poker game. For two nights in a row he had won Longarm's money, and Longarm was getting just a little tired of it. Besides, the man, a visitor to the area, had a kind of smart-aleck smirk about him that Longarm didn't care for one little bit. And then there was the question of what the man was doing in Mason County just when the outlaw gang was running wild. It was, Longarm thought, about time he and the stranger had a little talk.

Longarm made a meal out of steak, mashed potatoes, squash, and green beans. Even though it was late in the season, the vegetable gardens of the area seemed to be productive. He paid his score with a silver dollar, and then walked next door to the Elite. He came in through the double doors and stood for a moment looking around. The place was fuller than usual, and the buzz of talk was at a higher level. He glanced toward a table in a back corner. He could see that the game he liked had already started. From where he stood he counted heads.

Including the casually arrogant stranger named Austin Davis, there were five players. He wasn't surprised that there was a seat open since it was the highest-priced game in the saloon, dollar ante, pot limit on the bets.

He got a double whiskey at the bar and then made his way through the smoke and the drinkers to the table. The available seat was almost against the back wall. As Longarm came up, the man named Austin Davis looked up from his cards and nodded toward the chair. "There's your seat. I told the boys you'd be along and I know that deputy U.S. marshals always like to sit with their backs to the back wall."

Longarm gave him an amused glance and sat down, sipping at his whiskey as he did. He glanced over at Davis. The man was something of a dresser, in a casual way. He wore a soft black leather vest, a black flat-crowned hat, and a white silk shirt open at the collar. He couldn't see them, but Longarm knew that he most likely had on tan twill pants and that his boots would be shined to a gloss. Davis wore a gunbelt the way a professional or anyone who needed to get at his weapon in a hurry wore it. He also wore a cutaway holster. It wasn't much good at keeping a gun in place if you got to rolling around on the floor, but it made getting a gun out faster a hell of a lot easier.

Longarm nodded at Davis. "I take it, Mister Davis, that you have nothing on your conscience that would cause you to take such precautionary steps as to where you sat?"

Davis said to the dealer, "Take two." He pitched two cards into the discard pile, received the two in return, and shuffled them around in his hand. He finally looked at his cards, easing the new cards into his view slowly and carefully behind his shielding hands. In answer to Longarm's question he said, "You might be making a presumption there, Marshal. Let's just say I ain't done nothing around here in the last day or two that would cause me to be extra careful." He counted some bills off his stack and threw them in the middle of the table, where there were already several bills. "Bet twenty dollars."

The man to Davis's left protested. "Hell, we playin' pot limit. They ain't but five dollars in the damn pot."

"Oh!" Davis said. He gave Longarm a slight smile as he pulled back fifteen dollars. "Sorry, gentlemen. Guess I got excited."

Longarm shook his head. It was one of the oldest tricks in poker. Austin Davis had known how much he could bet and that he would be called to pull back money. But it would stick in the other players' minds that he had, obviously, a hand that he'd been eager to bet twenty dollars on. It was what was known as a delayed bluff. His real bluff would come on the next bet. Longarm wished he was in the hand. He was almost certain that Davis probably had very little. He'd kept three cards, but Longarm was pretty sure that was only for effect. He might have a pair of jacks or such, and had held a third card for a kicker to make it seem like he had three of a kind. As Longarm waited for the next deal and watched the play, his palms fairly itched. He wished to hell he was in the hand, even with nothing more than a pair of kings. He felt damn sure it would beat whatever Austin Davis had.

The man who had opened bet a cautious five dollars after all the players had taken their cards. As always they were playing dealer's choice, and the dealer had dealt a hand of five-card draw, jacks or better to open.

Austin Davis called the five-dollar bet and raised twenty dollars. The man to his left, Amos Goustwhite, immediately folded. The Goustwhites, Longarm knew, were one of the six or seven largest families around the county. He knew the man was kin to Bodenheimer, but he wasn't sure how.

He watched the play. The next player along the table

hesitated, looked at his cards, and folded. Only the opener, a man Longarm didn't know, gave the raise thought. He looked at his cards, and then he looked at the pot, and then he looked at Austin Davis. Davis watched him with amused eyes, then said, "Jump in there. It's only recreation."

The man frowned. He picked up a twenty-dollar bill, hesitated, looked at Austin Davis again, and then slammed the money in the middle of the pot. He said, "Dammit, I know you are bluffing. You are trying to buy this pot and I ain't letting you." He showed his hand. "I opened with a pair of queens and I caught a pair of jacks. Beat two pair if you can."

Austin Davis shook his head. "Well, Orville, them is mighty nice cards. Very pretty. And big! I mean they got paint all over them. I can't match that."

The man he'd called Orville said, "What in hell have you got, dammit?"

Davis gave him an amused look. "Mine are small, but I got several of them." He showed his hand. "Three sixes."

"Sonofabitch!" the man said, and slammed his hand down on the table. "I thought fer sure you was fakin'."

As he raked in the pot Austin looked over at Longarm and said, "What about you, Marshal? Did you think I was bluffing?"

Longarm gave him a look. He was an arrogant son of a bitch, all right. In spite of that, Longarm felt he could like the man if only he could finally beat him at poker. Davis was trimly built, one of those men, Longarm thought, who were a hell of a lot stronger than you'd thought once you got hold of them. He was handsome, Longarm reckoned, in a way that women found pleasing. Longarm just considered the man a little too well ordered in his dress and his features. A little dirt, Longarm thought, would look well on the man.

He didn't answer Davis directly, just yawned and said,

"I wasn't really paying any attention."

Davis laughed lightly. "I'm sure you weren't, Marshal. No, I wouldn't think you were a man who paid much attention to what went on around you."

To cover his irritation Longarm reached in his pocket and came out with his money. He counted off a hundred dollars, put that on the table in front of him, and put the rest of his roll back in his pocket. He could see that Davis had been doing well, but surprisingly, it was Amos Goustwhite who seemed to have the biggest pile in front of him. It looked to be over a hundred dollars, which was a pretty good stake for anyone else but Austin Davis.

They played a couple of hands, neither of which Longarm was able to be a part of because of the cards he'd drawn. Then the deal passed to Goustwhite. Longarm watched as the player shuffled the cards and set them to his right, in front of Austin Davis, to be cut. Davis took the top half of the cards off and cut them toward Goustwhite. Just as Goustwhite put his right hand out to complete the cut and join the two halves, he nodded toward the front of the saloon and said, "Look yonder who is coming."

Longarm, like every player at the table, started to glance toward the door. But out of the left corner of his eye he saw a blur of motion. He cut his eyes back in time to see Austin Davis smash the barrel of his revolver down across Goustwhite's forearm. Goustwhite screamed, and the other players switched their attention back to the table. They stared in disbelief as, in one motion, Austin Davis moved the barrel of his revolver off Goustwhite's arm and stuck the muzzle in the man's neck, right under his ear. Davis said, "All right, Amos, now take your damn hand off that deck. Real slow and careful or I'll blow your brains on the ceiling."

Goustwhite was screaming in pain, but he was mindful of the revolver muzzle rammed up under his chin.

One or two of the other players called out for Longarm to do something, to stop Austin Davis from killing the man. But Longarm simply watched. He had the feeling that Davis knew what he was doing and was doing it on purpose.

Goustwhite said in a high, wailing voice, "You've broke my arm! You crazy sonofabitch, you've broke my arm plumb off!"

Davis jabbed him harder with the muzzle of his pistol. "Move your damn hand, Amos. I'll give you one more warning. Get it off them cards or I'll break something else."

Still moaning and crying, Goustwhite reached across his body with his left hand, picked up his right arm and hand, and laid them carefully on the table before him. He looked up at the ceiling, his eyes shut against the pain. He said, "Marshal, the man nearly has kilt me! I want him arrested."

Austin Davis slowly lowered his revolver and transferred it to his left hand. He kept the muzzle dug in Goustwhite's side and said, "This man has been making a false cut. I noticed him at it last night. But I waited until now, when Marshal Long was here, to call him on it."

Davis had the other players' attention. He said, "He give me the cards to cut. I cut them. But just as he went to put them back together, he called our attention away from the table. I pretended to look, but instead, I was watching his hand. He put the cards back together exactly as they had been before he shuffled them. I think he stacked the cards before the cut, while he was shuffling. When he put them back the same way he left them set up to deal himself a good hand. He had already called for five-card draw. I will be greatly surprised if he don't have at least three of a kind. In fact, if he doesn't, I'll give him five hundred dollars. That sound fair?"

The other men were nodding. Longarm didn't say

anything. Davis looked at him. "Well, Marshal?"

Longarm shrugged. "Why don't you let him whack you across the forearm with his pistol?"

Davis grinned, his eyes dancing. "Instead of the five hundred or in addition to it?"

"In addition to it."

"Fine."

One of the players said, "Hell, deal them out. Let us see."

Goustwhite suddenly made a sound and tried to rise. "I got to go see a doctor. I feel awful."

Davis jabbed him hard with his revolver. "Sit down, Amos. That blow on your arm is at least three feet from your heart. You'll live."

Goustwhite slowly settled back in his chair, but he cradled his hurt forearm to his chest and rocked slowly back and forth, moaning as he did.

"Turn those cards, Davis," Longarm said.

Austin Davis put out his right hand to the deck. It had sluffed off a little, and he squared it with nimble fingers. Then he began dealing the cards around. On the first card, dealing from Goustwhite's position, Goustwhite drew a king. On the second round of cards Goustwhite drew another king. The players were slowly starting to cuss. As Davis dealt the third round Goustwhite again tried to rise. The man on his other side put his hand on Goustwhite's shoulder and shoved him back in the chair. He said, "Sit down. Let's see what that third card is."

On the third card Goustwhite drew a third king. Austin Davis stopped and slouched back in his chair. He slowly transferred his revolver to his right hand and then shoved the pistol home in its holster. He said, "Any point in dealing on? He's kind of a clumsy crook. I don't reckon he could have stacked the deck any deeper than three down. But three of a kind will win most pots in draw poker."

One of the men looked at Longarm. "What had we ought to do, Marshal?"

Longarm shrugged. "I'm not a marshal right now. My badge is in my pocket. I'm just a poker player."

Austin Davis said, "I know what to do. He cheated to win money. Now he is going to lose it for the same reason." He reached over in front of Goustwhite and picked up the man's stake.

Between groans, Goustwhite looked around and said, almost sobbing, "Some of that is my start money. They is seventy dollar of my own money in thar'."

Austin Davis was undeterred. He said, "About what you won last night." He glanced up at Goustwhite. "Now I wish to hell I'd hit you harder. You damn near won as much as I did last night, and that irritates the hell out of me."

Goustwhite said, clutching his arm, "Who knows you didn't cheat?"

Davis fixed him with a look. "You are a damn fool. The day I have to cheat to beat the likes of you is the day I quit poker. Now get the hell out of here, before I quit being so merciful."

Goustwhite slowly stood up. But before he could move Davis shot out his left hand and grabbed a fistful of the man's shirt. He pulled Goustwhite back a little and said, "Listen, Amos, when you get to the middle of the room I want you to sing out and announce to the crowd that you are a card cheat. You don't, I'm liable to break your other damn arm."

Goustwhite looked back at him, his face filled with pain and hate. He jerked his shirt loose and started making his way through the crowd.

Longarm said to Davis, "I'll bet you ten dollars he doesn't do it."

Davis gave him a small smile. "I don't care if he does or not. Within an hour everyone will know he's crooked."

"You've made an enemy I reckon."

Davis smiled. "So has he." Then he turned to the money. He counted it swiftly. "Looks like a hundred and thirty-five." He started peeling off money and dropping it in front of each man. He said, "That's twenty-five apiece for the four of you and thirty-five for me because I caught him and because that's the easiest way to divide it up." He laughed.

Longarm looked at the bills in front of him. He pushed them back to the middle of the table. "That ain't mine. He didn't win nothing off me. I only been here for a couple of hands."

Davis looked at him. "No, but he won it off you last night. He was doing the same thing. I just wasn't sure until tonight."

Longarm looked at him evenly. "Nevertheless," he said. He left the twenty-five dollars where it was. In the middle of the pot.

Austin Davis said, "Do I gather that you disapproved of what I done, Marshal?"

Longarm turned his eyes full on the man. "Mister Davis, when you do something I disapprove of, you won't have to ask."

Davis challenged him back. "Then why don't you take the money? You figure you are better than us?"

"You, for sure. The others I don't know about. Maybe I'm just angry because I didn't catch the bastard. The money is in the pot. We'll play for it this hand. I'll win it anyway. Just like I intend to have most of your money before the night is out. Now deal, dammit."

Austin Davis laughed low in his throat. "You may get some of my money, but not the way you play poker."

Longarm leaned back in his chair. "Mister Davis, I believe me and you are going to have us a talk in the not-too-distant future."

Davis was watching the deal go around. He said, "Always happy to help the law, Marshal. Especially the federal law. I'll try and make some time late tomorrow and have a talk with you. Be glad to give you the benefit of my experience.''

They played without much talk for the next four hours. At the end of a hand Longarm sat back in his chair and yawned and then counted his money. He was up about sixty dollars. The players had changed several times except for him and Austin Davis. He could not tell how much Davis was winning, but he was irked to think it was more than sixty dollars. Several times he'd almost had Davis trapped in a hand when he, Longarm, knew that he had the best cards. But each time something had warned Davis, and he had dropped out before the final bet. And in the same way, Longarm had eluded the net that Austin Davis had several times spread for *him*. Still, it seemed that, once again, Davis was going to be the big winner.

Longarm got out his watch and looked at it. It was five minutes to midnight. He stood up and shoved his roll of bills in his pocket. Austin Davis looked up. ''You leaving us? So early? Hell, it's just the shank of the evening.''

''Glad you think so because you're coming too.''

Davis said, ''Marshal, I am right happy here.''

Longarm crooked his finger. ''Get your money. Me an' you are going to have that talk.''

''What if I ain't ready to talk?''

Longarm shrugged. ''It's all the same to me. One way will be easier on you, that's all. But you will be coming along.''

Davis said, ''Well, since you've been so nice about it and all. How can I refuse an invitation so elegantly put.'' He stood up and began gathering up his money. He looked around the table. ''Gentlemen, if I disappear you will all remember this moment, will you not?''

One of them said, "All I know is you are leaving with most of my money. Hell, Marshal, you're a winner too."

Longarm looked at him. He said, "Why, hell, yes, I'm winning. That's the point of the game, you damn fool."

Davis said, "See, Jack? That's why you always lose your money. You never had anyone explain the point of the game to you before."

Longarm said, "Let's go."

Davis said, "Am I under arrest, Marshal?"

Longarm said, "Not yet, Davis, but the night is young."

Chapter 4

They walked the short distance to Longarm's hotel. Austin Davis said, "Where in hell are we going?"

"We're going somewhere quiet to have a talk. My hotel room."

"What if I don't want to have a talk?"

Longarm shrugged. "Then I reckon you go on back to the poker game and find out how many kinfolks Amos Goustwhite has got and how many of them have heard about you breaking his arm."

"Hell, I ain't afraid of none of these cross-eyed inbred jackasses."

"How about a couple dozen of them? All backshooters and bushwhackers?"

Davis was quiet for a few steps. Then he said, "Well, I don't reckon it will hurt to come along and hear what you've got to say. You got any decent whiskey?"

"I got a little of the finest Maryland whiskey made, but I ain't going to waste it on you. I got some other been in a bottle just about as long as it's been called whiskey. You can have some of that."

They were about to enter the hotel. Davis said, "I always like to deal with a generous man."

As they walked through the small lobby Longarm said, "Are you wanted?"

"By the law, no. Maybe by a few husbands. Why? What the hell difference does it make? There's about a half a dozen or more wanted men in this county and you ain't laid a finger on none of them. Hell, I wouldn't be surprised wasn't one or two of them in that saloon tonight."

Longarm was unlocking the door to his room. He shoved it open so Davis could enter and said, "What makes you think that? You referring to the Shaker bunch?"

Austin Davis went into the room and looked around. He shrugged his shoulders. "Hell, why not? From what I've been able to pick up they are tied mighty close to a lot of people around here."

"Sit down," Longarm said. He made a motion at a small round table set at one end of the room. There were three wooden chairs around it. Longarm sat in one and Austin Davis took another. There was a half a quart of his Maryland whiskey sitting in the middle of the table along with several glasses. Longarm uncorked the bottle, took up a glass, poured it half full, and shoved it across to Davis. He did the same for himself, and they made a toast and then both took a good drink. Austin Davis looked at his glass and said, "If this is green whiskey, then I want to know where I can buy a whole bunch of it."

Longarm lounged back in his chair. "I made a mistake. I forgot I left the good stuff out."

Davis took another drink and wiped the back of his hand across his mouth. "Well, out with it, Marshal. I know you ain't giving this whiskey away to folks who irritate you for no good reason."

"Who said you irritate me?"

"I got eyes. Besides, I irritate most folks." He chuckled. "I don't know why, though. I'm just trying to get along."

Longarm sipped at his whiskey, studying Davis over the rim of his glass. He needed some help from someone with a very special talent, and this insolent man who was so cocksure, and probably with good reason, just might be what he was looking for. "Davis," he said, "it is hard to tell when you are bluffing. I noticed that in the poker game. You do it well."

"Do what well?"

"Keep the other players off balance. You make it so they never feel quite comfortable about what you are up to."

"Ain't that the point?"

"You that good away from the poker table?"

Davis took a sip of whiskey and set his glass down. "I'm alive, ain't I?"

"Where you from?"

Davis shrugged. "Oh, different places. I move around a lot. I guess if you could say one area, it would be the border." He glanced up at Longarm. "You know the border. A place of sunny climes filled with shady characters."

"Any one place?"

Davis stiffled a yawn. " 'Scuse me. Oh, not really. I guess if I was pressed I'd say Del Rio, but what is true today might not be true tomorrow. You got any reason for this big interest you are taking in me?"

"Maybe. What the hell you doing way off up here, hundred and fifty miles from Del Rio. At least."

Davis shrugged. "Maybe I wasn't in Del Rio when I started this way. Maybe I was closer."

"That still don't tell me what you are doing here."

Davis finished his drink and set his empty glass on the table. Longarm shoved the bottle over to him and watched while he refilled his glass. Davis took the time to take a sip of his new drink before speaking. "What makes that your business?'' he said.

"The fact that there is an outlaw gang operating around here and a man in town to act as their eyes and ears would be handy. You're a stranger. Best I can figure it, you came to town about two days after I did.''

Austin Davis laughed. "Three, if you want to be accurate about the matter.''

"All right, three then. Now what brings you to these parts? I can't see much here would interest a man such as yourself.''

Davis gave him a quick look. "Hold on there. What do you mean, 'a man such as yourself'? Exactly how have you got me pegged?''

Longarm pursed his lips. After a moment's thought he said, "Well, you ain't exactly a working cowboy. And ain't nobody going to mistake you for a preacher. A fool looking to get killed might think you are on the soft side. You ain't short of coin. You are either a gambler or a man who uses a gun for something other than sporting purposes. So answer the question.''

Davis laced his fingers behind his head and leaned back in his chair. "I reckon, to be exact about the matter, you could say I'm down here to do a little gleaning.''

Longarm frowned. "Gleaning? How is that?''

Austin Davis leaned forward and took up his glass. He had another drink and then stared at the amber-colored whiskey. " 'Bout a couple of weeks ago,'' he said, "I was up from the border. Hanging around in Kimble County, near Junction City. Of course I'd been hearing about these goings-on for at least a year, this foolishness in Mason County. I'd been meaning to look into it, and then I heard you were here.'' He gave Longarm the flicker of a smile. "Didn't know you was famous, did you, Marshal Long. Longarm. The long arm of the law.''

"Get to your point.''

Davis shrugged. "It's pretty simple. There is wanted

55

paper out on several of the boys in that gang. Not big money, five hundred to a thousand. That bank in Junction has put that much on the head of any man involved in their robbery. Anyway . . ." He shrugged again. "Anyway, I figured you intended to give the tree a pretty good shake. I just figured to be on hand and pick up any loose apples might be laying around on the ground. Do a little gleaning."

"So you are a bounty hunter."

Davis shook his head. "No, that ain't exactly right. If you've got to put a name to my main vocation, I'd reckon you could call me a gambler. But only with money. I am adverse to gambling with my hide turning bullets. I have taken a few boys in for the money on their heads, but it was mainly because they more or less dropped into my lap. I ain't *never* gone around making a habit out of chasing folks who didn't want to be chased and would put a hole through you for your troubles." He gave Longarm a careless smile. "Like I said, I was here doing some gleaning, some picking up after. I figured to let you do the dangerous work and I'd take what was left."

Longarm studied him a long moment. "I got a hunch about you, Davis. I think you like to keep folks off guard. I think you've put your hide on the line a few more times than you are admitting to me."

Davis yawned. "You think what you want to, Longarm. Don't make no difference to me. But if you've got me pegged as being in with this outfit that's doing the robbinng around here, you can think again. When I found out they had robbed the auction barn, I knew right then and there they wasn't going to last much longer, not as dumb as they appear to be. Nosir, I'd just as soon you wouldn't lump me in with no outfit that dumb."

Longarm said, "Raise your right hand, Davis."

Austin Davis looked startled. He glanced at Longarm. "What for? I don't need to go outside."

"Don't be an asshole. Raise your right hand. I am going to swear you in as a provisional deputy U.S. marshal."

Davis gave him a mild look. "Like hell you are."

"Why not?"

"All the use of a badge is that it makes a good target. No, thank you, sir."

"Listen, Davis, as a federal officer I can procure anything that belongs to the federal government, all the way from horses and mules to wagons and soldiers. You are a citizen of the United States. That means I can procure you."

"You ain't drafting me."

"You ever been called for jury duty?"

"Who hasn't. But it ain't the same."

"It's exactly the same. The government is calling upon you to do your duty. Now raise your right hand. If you don't, I'm going to stick you in a jail cell with the sheriff and his deputies."

Davis looked interested. "You arrested the sheriff?"

"And his two blood-kin deputies."

"What for?"

"For collusion, for accessory, for irritating the hell out of me by playing me for a fool. What difference does it make."

Davis looked impressed. "Well, well. Sounds to me like you are making progress." He glanced at Longarm. "But I still don't want no badge."

"You ain't going to get no badge," Longarm said. "Hell, I don't even wear mine half the time. And you ain't going to tell nobody that you've been sworn in. I've got a special job for you."

"Yeah? What is it?"

"I reckon you take yourself for a hell of a hand with the ladies."

Davis gave Longarm his slightly arrogant, slightly amused smile. He said easily, "Oh, I reckon I could get some testimonial letters if it got right down to it.''

Longarm gave him a grim look. "I wouldn't be taking all this with such a light heart. It might get a little rough in places."

"Did I give that impression? Hell, Marshal, you misunderstand me. I am the most serious and humble of men."

"Bullshit. If there was anybody else I wouldn't even throw a rock at you. But I need some help. Now raise your damn right hand."

Davis frowned slightly, but he slowly put his hand in the air. "Like this?"

"Like anyway you want. Do you swear to abide by the rules and conditions of the Marshals' Service, so help you on your oath?"

"Hell, I don't know what they are."

"Dammit, Davis, just say yes."

"All right, yes. What now?"

"For openers you can put your hand down. You going to look damn silly walking around like that for the rest of your life."

"Is that it? Is that all?"

"Yeah, you are now a provisional deputy U.S. marshal, subject to all the laws and conditions of that office."

"What does that mean?"

"For one thing, it means that there are more than just several things you better do, and several you better not do. Some can get you in jail, a few can get you hung."

Davis's eyes got wide. "Oh, hell, that was exactly what I wanted to hear. Oh, hell, yes. That's the kind of news makes a man glad he joined up. Exactly what are you talking about."

"You are now sworn to uphold the laws of the United States. It means you better do your duty, you better not get caught disobeying any orders, it means you better uphold the law, and it means you better not get caught with any money in your pockets ain't supposed to be there.''

Davis reached out and poured himself another drink. ''What's the pay?''

''Three dollars a day. Out of that you outfit yourself, furnish your own mount, your own cartridges and arms, and find food and fodder for yourself and your animals. How you shelter yourself is not a concern of the government.''

Davis nodded. ''Sounds fair to me. Hell, if a man had the money behind him, he could work at such a job for a good long while before he went broke.''

Longarm said dryly, ''Glad you are taking it so well.''

Austin Davis gave him a look. ''Marshal, I don't exactly understand why you picked me for this job unless you think there is an outstanding chance of me getting killed. I've had the impression right along that you didn't much care for me. Might even say you disapprove of me.''

Longarm gave him a grimace. ''You're so damn neat, Davis! Hell, you don't look like you've ever had a speck of dirt on you. I've been encountering you for three, maybe four days and you ain't never got a hair out of place. You are always shaved, your pants are pressed and your shirt. Your boots are shined. Hell, your damn fingernails are even clean. Ain't you ever rolled around in the dust and mud?''

Davis laughed mildly. ''Maybe that's the reason I'm so neat now. But that ain't what we are talking about right now. You've asked me to do some kind of job. You ain't told me what it is yet.''

Longarm frowned and poured himself a drink. He sat, sipping at it slowly while he tried to think. It wasn't an easy proposition to put forth. Finally he said, ''You ever heard of ol' Dalton Diver? Lives here.''

Davis thought a moment and then shook his head. ''Not that I recollect.''

"Well, he's got a passel of daughters and he makes a business of marrying them off. The best I can find out he's married four of them into that gang. So far it don't appear to have been lucky for the men involved. Best I can count, three of them have been killed."

Austin Davis snapped his fingers. "Yeah. Yeah. Yeah, I heard about him. In the saloon. I thought somebody was pulling my leg."

Longarm shook his head. "Ain't no kidding about it. If what little I've heard is true, I got to believe it ties in somehow." As best he could, with what little he knew, Longarm told Austin Davis about the sisters and their connections with the outlaws and about Dalton Diver's method of marrying or "selling" off his daughters.

When he was through, Davis shook his head. "That's the damnedest thing I ever heard. Yeah, I'd say there's got to be some kind of connection. Either that or it's the biggest coincidence that ever came down the pike. How do you want to play it?"

Longarm picked up his glass of whiskey and thought a moment. "Thing is, I don't know enough to say what to do. All I know is that I can't spark more than one of them girls at a time. They're sisters, don't you see, and a man that was doubling around on them would get caught in nothing flat. I already got this Hannah in my gunsights, so I figure to proceed along that line and see what turns up."

"You got one in mind for me?"

"Yeah. That Rebeccah. According to Hannah she married a Lester Gaskamp who was supposed to be the leader of the bunch at the time. He was killed right off and old Dalton had him another daughter ready for sale."

Austin Davis said, "Seems like the bride price is a touch high for what the husbands get."

"Near as I can figure, they don't get nothing."

"What does this Rebeccah look like?"

"If she looks anything like Hannah, she'll make your pistol stand up and dance."

Davis smiled slowly. "I could stand a little of that."

Longarm said sharply, "Your main duty is to try and pump her dry. You are after information."

"What kind of information?"

Longarm shook his head. "I don't know. I feel sure that Bodenheimer has got to be tied to that gang in some ways, but I got the same feeling about Dalton Diver."

"Well, his daughters ain't going to give him away if that is what you are hoping for."

"You mean you can't raise a woman to a level of excitement that she ain't aware of what she's saying?"

"I can do that, yes. But what she is saying don't generally have nothing to do with an outlaw gang and her daddy. And I doubt seriously that you can either."

Longarm grimaced. "I reckon we are just going to have to piece together what little bits of information we can. Listen, you've been here as a civilian. Likely folks will talk freer around you than they will me. What have you heard? It strikes me that the folks around here are damned unconcerned about having such an outfit operating here so openly for so much time. It is unnatural."

"I can't put a finger on any one thing," Davis said. "Though I agree with you that it is unnatural. The local citizenry seems to be uninterested or at least unworried. If I had a gang of cutthroats running loose, I'd be hollering to the law left and right. I was in the saloon when word come in that the auction barn had been robbed. So far as I know, that's the first piece of business has been done inside the county lines. But you'd of thought it had happened in Louisiana the way folks took it. Of course that saloon crowd ain't going to get too excited about anything unless the robbers was to come in and steal the beer and whiskey straight out of their glasses."

Longarm got out a cigar and lit it. When it was drawing good he said, "Well, I got Bodenheimer locked up.

If he is going to tell me anything, it's going to be after he has baked behind those bars for a time. But to tell you the truth, I don't think the sonofabitch knows much. If I was a bandit with a lick of brains, I wouldn't tell Bodenheimer anything. Just pay him off. No, there is somebody else making this thing work. I got to figure it is Dalton Diver, and the only way I know to get at him is through his daughters.''

"Exactly how am I supposed to approach this daughter of his? Rebeccah you said her name was?''

Longarm stood up and stretched. "I don't know. Why don't you knock on my door in the morning and we'll go eat some breakfast. It's near two o'clock.''

Austin Davis got up. "What time?''

"Whatever time you get up and get hungry. We don't keep no schedule in this business. And I ain't got to tell you again, do I, to keep this deputy marshal business to yourself.''

"No. Of course not.''

"Folks you've met—do they know you're bounty hunting?''

Davis frowned. "That ain't something you go around advertising. All a bounty hunter is is a man with some wanted paper in his pocket looking for some faces or bodies to go with the paper. Hell, anybody can do it. The trick is to collect the money. It ain't something it pays to advertise about.''

"Well, get on out of here." Longarm yawned. "I will say this one more thing, Davis. I ain't in the habit of picking up help like this. I'm taking a risk with you.''

Austin Davis made a droll face. "Yeah, I see how you're taking a hell of a risk. Let's see, I ain't got no badge, no papers, no appointment, nothing but a conversation held with a man over whiskey and late hours. Yeah, you're the one taking the risk, all right. I can see that.''

"You got a smart answer for everything?''

"Only when the conversation takes a turn on the dumb side." He turned and started to open the door. Longarm's voice stopped him. He looked back. "What?"

Longarm said, "I don't think you fetched up to what I meant about them little flowers waiting to have their petals plucked. If Hannah is right, then the woman you are going to go sniffing around ain't been tested yet."

Davis laughed. "Hell, I don't believe you. By your own admission you was about to help little Hannah out of her problem, and she'd only been married a little better than a month. Rebeccah has been married two years. Or widowed two years. I got to believe that some buck has come along to show her when to ride and when to get off."

Longarm took a pull on his cigar. "Hannah said her mother's advice was to wait until a man come along that she took a shine to and then put him to work. I ain't all that sure that man has come along for Rebeccah, not seeing I'm tied up with Hannah and can't get free. I would reckon Rebeccah has got the same high standards as Hannah. I'm hoping you can fill the bill. But that's all I'm doing. Hoping."

"Just keep your hopes a-going, my friend. I'll handle the rest of it."

"You know you got to handle a virgin kind of careful. Can't push them along too fast. A little teaching might be in order. That is, if you know anything about the subject yourself."

Austin Davis stood there, his hand slowly turning the doorknob back and forth. "You will rag a fellow, won't you, Longarm. If you need me to give you some pointers with Hannah, why don't you just up and ask instead of beating around the bush like you are doing. By your own mouth you couldn't handle matters this afternoon. Made up some story about being called away by the sheriff. Is that the reason you arrested him? He didn't interrupt you earlier?''

Longarm gave him a sour look. "Get on out of here, Davis. Be the last time I waste my breath giving you advice."

Austin Davis laughed and went through the door, closing it behind him. Longarm walked over and turned the key in the lock. He very seldom bothered with that sort of thing, but he had an uneasy feeling about his situation. He didn't ever recollect being in a place where he had a harder time telling who was who and who was on which side of the law. He shook his head, went over, sat down on the side of the bed, and started taking off his boots. It was getting to be one too many for him. He wondered whether he should have a talk with Bodenheimer the first thing in the morning or go out and work on Hannah. The prospect of working on Hannah certainly presented a much more appealing picture, but he thought he ought to pass by and make sure Bodenheimer and his kin were still under lock and key. Melvin Purliss did not strike him as the most reliable jailer he'd ever seen. He yawned and started undressing. It had been a long day.

Longarm came out of the sheriff's office and mounted his horse. He turned away and rode south across the front of the courthouse, and then turned east toward the river and Hannah's cabin. The morning air was fresh and crisp, with the smell of fall in it. Mason, he decided, was a pretty little town, in spite of the people that lived there. As he rode around the two-story courthouse built of country rock, with a big yard shaded by pecan trees, he couldn't help but speculate that people could get themselves in more trouble in five minutes than they could get out of in a lifetime. Breaking the law just wasn't a good play. Even if you didn't get caught, there'd be people in your life who would know you were crooked, and most folks had a conscience to nag them. And if you got caught, well, the law could be a hell of a lot tougher on you than any conscience.

He turned his head to look back at the sheriff's office just before it was obscured by the courthouse. The town was built around the square, with shops and stores and residences on every side. The sheriff's office was on the north side, just to the right and across the street as you came out of the courthouse. Bodenheimer had been as angry as an ignorant, guilty man could be. He had insisted that Longarm release him and his deputies instantly, and do something to restore him in the esteem of the townspeople. Longarm had replied that he'd be glad to turn them loose the minute that Bodenheimer could explain, to Longarm's satisfaction, how a gang of outlaws had managed to operate and hide out in his fairly small county. Longarm had said, "I don't know of a magistrate or law officer of any consequence whatsoever, or of any sense or with the slightest bit of intelligence, who wouldn't have to conclude that you have been in cahoots with the bandits, if not from the start, then very shortly thereafter. It's either that, or you are the most ignorant man who ever wore a badge anywhere at any time."

Bodenheimer had continued to bluster and glower, but it hadn't done him any good. The only one of the deputies who'd had anything to say had been Melvin Purliss, and he had been worried if what he was doing was right and legal. He'd said, "Sheriff Bodenheimer says if I don't let him out at once, he's gonna lock me up the minute he gets out and hang me the next day. Marshal, you shore this is right? You ain't got no idea the number of people been by here askin' questions and not believin' me when I tell them I ain't got the say in this situation. They can't see, federal marshal or not, how you come to have the right to lock up their sheriff."

Longarm had assured the deputy that, as a federal

marshal, he could indeed arrest a deputy or a sheriff or any other county or state or territorial official he chose. He'd said, "Now a judge can come along and say they had not ought to have been arrested, but until a judge comes along and says different, Bodenheimer and his kindred are arrested and are going to stay that way. And if you let anything happen to them, such as getting loose, you are going to be in pretty bad shape."

That had scared Purliss more than Longarm had meant, so he'd been forced to spend a little time bolstering up the deputy. He'd ridden away certain in his mind that it was going to take more than one night in jail to get Bodenheimer to come around to Longarm's way of thinking. Until then he was going to have to enjoy the county's cooking and shelter.

Longarm got out of the town and picked up the little road that led down to the river. He and Austin Davis had not had as much to talk about as he'd thought. Most of what he'd had to say had been to warn the gambler about being careful how he asked questions. Longarm had said, "Near as I can make out, the only person you can trust in this county is me, and I wouldn't be all that sure about me. You go to pressing that Rebeccah in the wrong way, and she is liable to squawk to someone and you are going to find yourself on the wrong end of a bushwhacker's bullet. Just concentrate on getting the clothes off her in the early going."

Austin Davis had given him an innocent look, and said he was under the impression that it was for that task and that task alone that he had been hired. "If you are expecting me to be worrying myself with law work, you have got another think coming."

But Davis had said something else that had set Longarm to thinking. "I'm kind of a student of towns and townspeople on account of that's the way I make my living. I don't earn every dollar across the card table. A part of the time I'm available for any scheme, legally, that might come my way. And that generally involves the folks that live in a place. Have you noticed the number of men in this town who don't seem to do much except hang around the saloons or the barbershop or the blacksmith shop or just sit around the courthouse spitting and whittling?"

Longarm had thought about it. In truth the very same idea had occurred to him, but not being as familiar with small Texas towns as Davis was, he hadn't studied on it much. But now that Davis had brought it to his attention, he had to admit that there did indeed seem to be a lot of young and middle-aged men with no visible means of support.

Davis had said, "If they are farmers, it ain't laying-by time yet. In fact, it is harvest time. If they are raising cattle or sheep, this is a busy time for both, getting your animals set for winter. Yet here are all these men hanging around town and doing nothing but spending time and money."

Longarm had pursed his lips. "Are you thinking what I think you are thinking?"

"That the best way to hide is in plain sight?"

"Yeah, something like that. But there's only supposed to be a half a dozen or so in the gang. Maybe eight. Lot more men of the right age hanging around."

Davis had looked at him. "What about if they took turns."

Longarm had been about to take a bite of steak and eggs. He'd put his fork down. "That's a hell of an idea. But the doing of it . . ." He'd let the thought trail off and shaken his head. "Too many people would have to be able to keep their mouths shut to make it work."

"Keep their mouths shut to who? You are the first outside law to come in here since this business got cranked up. Who they going to keep their mouths shut to?"

It had made Longarm blink. The idea was overwhelming. Austin Davis was talking about a whole town, maybe even a whole county, cooperating on robbery and keeping it hidden. It was too fantastic to believe. Longarm had said, "You forget they robbed the auction barn."

"Yes, and how much talk did you hear about it afterward? Most of the hollering, according to you, took place at the auction barn itself, and most of those folks were from out of the county. I was in the saloon for several hours after it happened, and damn little got said. A whole hell of a lot of damn little. Amos Goustwhite and another man come in about three, three-thirty. Two hours after the robbery. I had opportunity to notice their horses were lathered up. I even choused them a little about holding a race and nobody won, both horses being too slow. I didn't think about it at the time, because I was too interested in getting Goustwhite in a game. But he and the man with him could just as easily have been in on that robbery and then circled around to make it into town. They'd have hurried so as to get there sooner than a man would coming from that distance. You think about it."

Longarm had frowned. "Truth be told, I don't want to think about it. Hell, if what you say is true, we'd have to arrest a thousand people."

"I'm not saying they are *all* in on it, maybe fifteen or twenty taking an active hand. But ain't you noticed what a prosperous little town this is? And there ain't that much around here to make for that much money coming in. Ain't a sawmill, ain't a cotton gin, ain't no real big ranches. Hell, the railroad don't even go through here. And you tell me about the bride price Old Man Diver is getting for his daughters. That is a revelation right there."

"But they robbed the auction barn."

"Maybe that was for your benefit. You ever think of

that? Besides, I asked some questions this morning. The Ownsbys don't live in Mason County. They live across the line closer to Llano than here."

Longarm had scowled. "Dammit, if I'd wanted somebody to make this job harder, I could have done it myself. That's the damnedest idea I ever heard of, and I ain't going to hear a word more on the subject."

But Austin Davis had said something else that had piqued Longarm's interest. As they were finishing up their breakfast with a last cup of coffee Davis had told him, "You know, I've heard the name Diver one other time and it ain't been that long ago. I was in Rock Springs, which is about halfway between Junction City and Eagle Pass, and I run into an hombre named Vince Diver. Looked to be a fairly capable man with a revolver. Didn't talk much, but didn't nobody mess with him."

"How old a man was he?"

Davis had shrugged. "Hard to say. On the youngish side, though he could have been thirty. But not much more. Also could have been twenty-five. I didn't have no reason to inquire."

Longarm said, "As I understand it, Dalton Diver ain't got no sons."

"Could be a brother. Maybe even a nephew or a cousin. You say this county is a-flood with the same blood."

"But no other Divers. Not that I know of."

"Just thought I'd mention it."

Now Longarm was picking his way along the little road between the low humps of the hills of the broken country. There weren't that many trees that abounded, the predominant types being post oak and mesquite, but there was enough mayhaw and wild plum and elm to give a nice variety and show some color as the leaves changed and fell to the ground. It was pretty country to look at, but hell to make a living in, Longarm thought.

But that brought him right back to what Austin Davis had said about the amount of money in the town and county when, by rights, they ought to be poor. Hell, it wasn't anything he could do something about, so his best hope was to plug away at the Diver girls and then Old Man Diver himself and Bodenheimer. Something would break.

The was a hill that Hannah's cabin backed up to. The road led around it. Once he was there, the cabin would be off to his left with the river some fifty or sixty yards straight ahead. He came around the last clump of bushes and opened up on the flat ground that ran down to the river. He was just at the point of reining his horse toward Hannah's cabin when he became aware of a man crossing the river, coming from the other side, heading toward Hannah's place. Longarm instantly stopped his horse, but he had already been seen. The man was about halfway across, some eighty or one hundred yards from Longarm. The marshal could see him clearly. He had a youngish face with a sparse mustache, and was wearing neat and well-kept clothes.

As Longarm stared, the man put his hand on the butt of his revolver. He did not draw it, but Longarm immediately wheeled his horse to face the man, giving him less of a target, and started his horse at a walk toward the river. For a second the man hesitated, and then he wheeled his horse and quickly rode back to the other bank, climbed it, and took off across the rolling prairie at a brisk lope. For a second, at the river's edge, Longarm was tempted to give chase. Instead, he wheeled his horse around and rode to the front of Hannah's cabin, calling her name as he neared. She came out the door almost before he could stop. He said, "Did you recognize that man crossing the river?"

She was wearing a lightweight blue frock and had her hair nicely brushed. She said, looking up at him with her big blue eyes, "Why, my yes, that was my husband. That was Gus Horne."

Chapter 5

Longarm stared at her. "You sure?"

"Well, land-a-mercies, yes. I never seen him all that much, but a girl don't forget the man she was wed to."

"Was he coming or going?"

"Coming, I reckon. First sight I had of him I was a-lookin' out the window. Lookin' for you, as a matter of fact, and then I seen him. And I says to myself, 'Why, look yonder, that looks like Gus Horne.' And it was. I didn't know what to think."

"Dammit!" Longarm said. He swung his horse around. The man had a good lead and the advantage of knowing the country. Behind him he could hear Hannah yelling. He looked back. "What?"

"Where you think you be goin'? You already late for supper last night. I done took a bath an' washed my clothes and all that."

"I'll be right back," he said. "Go in the house and sit real still and you won't mess your dress up."

Then he put his horse's hooves in the water and urged the animal across the swift-running water and the slick rocks. Fortunately, the land was flatter on the far side. It only rose into hills after a quarter of a mile. But still, Gus Horne had managed enough of a lead that he would

71

be hard to catch, and harder still to track over the rocky, stony ground.

The country at first was much more flat and open than he had expected. There was no sign of Gus Horne, but Longarm proceeded cautiously, eyeing the ground for sign while taking quick, sweeping looks around for any indication of an ambush. Now and again he caught sign of a hoof imprint in the short, cured grass. The sign led to the southeast, and he bore in that direction. Soon the ground was starting to rise quickly, heading for a line of short, hard-topped hills. He rode carefully, still searching ahead for any sign of Horne before glancing at the ground ahead. By the overhead sun he calculated it was noon. Apparently Gus Horne had been planning on dropping by to see his bride over lunch. Longarm wondered what had caused the man to make an appearance after all this time. He wondered if it had anything to do with the auction barn robbery or the arrest of Otis Bodenheimer.

But he broke off his musing as the trail led to the south and entered a broad, sandy rise heading toward some mesquite-topped hills. Off to his right was a jumble of rocks and brambles of weeds. The tracks were plain now, though they were beginning to veer toward the right, toward the rough cover on that side. A thought hit him that his quarry might be doubling back on him after giving him such plain sign to follow. At the instant of the thought, two things happened; his horse suddenly spooked to the left, and a slug thudded into the saddlehorn, throwing pieces of leather and wood in all directions. He heard the sound of the shot booming as he let himself fall backwards off the left side of his horse, drawing his revolver as he did.

He turned in the air. His head was toward the rear of his horse and he could see a line of weeds and rocks not ten yards off. He was not sure, but he thought he got off one shot before he hit the ground. He felt the thud as his chest landed first, but he had his arm out, his revolver aimed at the clump of weeds. He was thumbing back the hammer when a man suddenly stood up. He was holding a long-barreled revolver in his right hand. Longarm could see it was Gus Horne. He fired twice, aiming for the center of the man's chest. He saw the puff of dust from Horne's shirt, and then Horne went over backward, the gun slipping from his fingers as he fell. Longarm had the impression, lying in the dirt, that he'd seen a splotch of red on the man's shirt even before he'd fired the third time. But there had been no time to ask questions or to enter into negotiations. Horne was a bandit, he'd fired first, he was standing up, and he was armed. That was enough to warrant another shot.

The flat fall on the hard ground had knocked the breath out of Longarm. When he could, he got slowly to one knee and then eased himself to his feet, still gasping at the air. His horse had run off a few feet and was standing, his reins dangling, looking back at Longarm to see what all the commotion was about. Longarm wasn't worried. The horse was ground-reined and wouldn't go far.

Still with caution, he approached the line of bushes where Horne had been. He held his revolver out, the hammer cocked, as he walked forward. Then he was near enough that he could see the head, then the chest, and then the rest of the man. His white shirtfront was stained with two big splotches of blood. The high one appeared to have taken him in the heart or very near. The other was lower down, more of a gut shot. Longarm guessed it was the lower shot that had stopped him and the other that had killed him. He reckoned his third shot had gone wide. Still, it wasn't bad, two hits out of three, while falling off a horse.

He stood over the man. Horne was finished, all right. Longarm uncocked his revolver and shoved it in his holster. He looked around. The man's horse should be nearby. He walked a few yards into a mesquite thicket and saw a horse tied just ahead. Horne had done just as he'd thought, left him clear sign in the sandy tract and then ridden off into the weeds and rocks and doubled back to a bushwhacking position. His only mistake had been he'd used a revolver instead of a rifle, and then he'd had the bad luck of Longarm's horse spooking when it did. Although on recollection, Longarm wasn't so sure it was luck at all. In the dim recesses of his mind he seemed to remember hearing a horse neigh just before his own horse had reacted. His horse hadn't spooked so much as he'd tried to turn to see the horse that was calling to him. Horne's mistake had been tying his horse so close. Well, Longarm thought, all in all he wasn't a very smart bandit.

Longarm untied the animal and led him over to where Horne's body lay. The smell of the blood made the horse nervous, but Longarm quieted him and tied him to a bush near the body. But before he loaded Horne back across his horse, he took a moment to go through both sides of Horne's saddlebags. In one he found a leather wallet that had G.W. stamped on the front. He unfolded it and found quite a lot of currency. At least more than one would expect to find in the wallet of a man like Horne. There were some gold coins totaling about a hundred dollars, and nearly three times that much in paper currency. But what was of the most interest to Longarm was three checks made out to the County Line Auction Barn and signed by men he didn't know. One was marked for "six heifers" and was for $178. Another was for $98 and was noted to be for a "saddle horse." The third was for $226 and bore no legend as to what it had been written for. Longarm had no doubt that the checks had been stolen the day before from the auction barn. Ownsby had been particularly aggrieved that the robbers had taken checks as well as the cash. He'd said, "Hell, I can understand them taking the cash, but they scooped up the checks that folks had paid for their stock with. The checks ain't a peck of good to them damn robbers, because they are made out to the auction barn. They couldn't cash them at any bank in the country. But they was still of value to me. Must have been a thousand dollars worth, and that was money I could have put to use. Hell, just because they are crooked don't mean they have to be ignorant as well.''

Longarm put the wallet in his own saddlebags. He would consider all the money, especially the checks, as the property of the auction barn. He reckoned that Ownsby and his wife would be glad to get that much back at least.

Finally he addressed himself to the task of getting Horne up and across his saddle. Horne wasn't a particularly big man, but he was deadweight. It was with an effort that he got the man across his saddle, belly down, his hands hanging on one side, his boots on the other. Longarm had some cords in his saddlebag, and he used several lengths to tie the body securely in place. Horne's horse was still acting up, looking walleyed and jumping around, but Longarm calmed him and the animal gradually settled down.

He caught his own horse up, rode over to where Horne's horse was, caught up the reins, and started back toward the river. He was not sure if he should go by Hannah's or not. It seemed a little awkward to come by bearing her dead husband, but he wanted to make sure he had the right man. He calculated he'd hide Horne and his horse, go in and talk to Hannah, and if it was all right with her, get her to identify the body.

But as he came down to the river, leading Horne and his horse, he saw Hannah come out the front door of her cabin and wave at him and call out. He stopped the horses in midstream and said, in a loud voice, for her to go back in the cabin. "Hannah, I got a dead body back

75

there on that horse. You might not ought to get too close."

But instead of retreating, she walked down toward the river. "Is it Gus Horne?"

He grimaced. "I think so. I was going to get you to take a look. That is, if you wasn't too upset."

"Naw. I'm fine. Bring him right on up here. Hell, I don't even know the man. He don't mean nothing to me."

Somewhat reluctantly Longarm urged his horse forward, cleared the river, and stepped out onto the ground in front of the cabin. Hannah was still about forty yards off. She waited while he rode slowly to her. When she was still ten yards distant, he stopped his horse and dismounted. As she started forward, he put up his hand and stopped her. He said, "I didn't want to kill him, Hannah. He got in the first shot. Bullet hit my saddlehorn as you can see. I didn't have much chance to do other than what I did."

She shrugged. "I don't know anything about such matters. Bring him on up here."

Silently he led both horses forward and then stopped. With Hannah following him he went back to the trailing horse, took Gus Horne by the hair, and lifted his head so Hannah could see him clearly. Longarm said, "Well?"

She nodded. "Yeah, that be the man I married."

"Gus Horne?" He was still bothered by the G.W. stamped on the wallet.

She shrugged. "Hell, I don't know what his name really was. That was the one he give. But my sisters say a lot of them bandits got two or three names."

Longarm looked at her closely. "You ain't the least bit sorry he is dead?"

She laughed girlishly. "Gonna make Paw happy. Means he can sell me again. I guess this makes me a widow, huh?"

Longarm shook his head in some amazement. "Yeah, I reckon you could say that."

She smoothed the front of her dress and looked up at Longarm. Her voice was a little husky when she said, "I'm mighty glad you didn't get hurt none."

"So am I," he said.

She said, "You about ready to come in now? Now that you've got your work done?"

It took him so off balance he didn't know what to say for a moment. Finally he stammered out something about taking the body into town.

She gave him an innocent look. "Why?"

"Why?" He didn't know what to say. He finally replied, "Hannah, there are laws. I have just killed this man. I've got to get him into the undertaker's office and notify the authorities. It's the law."

"But you're the law."

"Look here, I need to get this man into town and get a tintype made of him. I assume this here town has got a photographer's shop?"

"I reckon. But you promised me you'd show up for supper yesterday and you never come."

"Hannah, honey . . ." He put his hands on her shoulders. "Don't you reckon I was dying to do just that? But that gang held up the auction barn yesterday and I had to go out there. By the time I was finished it was good and late." He started to tell her about Bodenheimer, but decided to hold his tongue. "Didn't you hear about the auction barn? That it was robbed?"

She shook her head. "Naw, I never hear anything out here 'less somebody comes by. But I wouldn't have cared nohow. All I cared about was you showing me what you said you would. That's why I don't want you going off now."

"But Hannah, I got to. I want to get a picture of this man and show it around. There's a chance he ain't even Gus Horne."

"I reckon I ought to know if it is Gus Horne or not. Hell, I married him, didn't I?"

"Yeah, but men have been known to change their names. Outlaws especially. You just said so. I need to get this body on into town."

She stamped her foot. "Now Marshal, you tie them horses up over there in the shade of them chinaberry trees and come on in the house."

Longarm took off his hat and wiped his brow with his forearm. For lack of something better to say, he said, "Hell, Hannah, it's Sunday."

"Well so what? Church is out, ain't it?"

Longarm put his hat on. "Hannah, I'll be back before you know it. I'm a law officer and I got my duty."

She pulled her lower lip down in a pout. "What about yore duty to me? You was gonna teach me."

He gave her a quick kiss. "And I still am. I'll be back before you can miss me. Hell, Hannah, I couldn't do my best with a dead man laying out here. I wouldn't be able to keep my mind on my business. You can see that."

She dug the toe of her slipper in the dirt. She was still wearing a pout. But she said, "Oh, I guess so. That's all girls ever get to do anyway, is wait. Wait and then wait some more. You be back before dark?"

"I'll do my dead-level best. Depends on what I find when I get to town. By the way, where does your daddy live?"

She gave him a look. "What you want to see him about?" Then her face suddenly brightened. "You going to ask for my hand? Now, with ol' Gus dead, wouldn't be nothing to stop you."

He gave her a grave look. "Hannah, there is nothing I would want more. But I can't. Federal marshals ain't allowed to marry."

"You could quit."

Her easy response, like a child, left him slightly staggered. He said, "Well, you see, it ain't that easy. You have to sign a . . . You have to sign a piece of paper says you'll stay on the job for so long. They won't let you quit."

"Oh." She put her hand to her breast. "Then you hurry in and hurry back."

Longarm swung up in the saddle, putting on his hat as he did. He said, "You never did say where your daddy lived."

She made a vague gesture to the northeast. "Oh, out the Llano road about four miles and then back east a couple. Almost down to the river. Got a real nice house. Part rock and part lumber and it's all painted white. Big place. Well, you'd figure that with the size family he had."

As he rode into town Longarm saw the remains of old Fort Mason. At one time it had been part of a chain of forts that had stretched from Fort Brown at the very southern tip of Texas clear across New Mexico to Fort Yuma in Arizona. The forts had been built to protect the settlers from Indian attacks, and as such, had been placed approximately a hundred miles apart, it being thought that cavalrymen could cover fifty miles in a day. Someone had told Longarm that Robert E. Lee had been in command of Fort Mason on the day he had left to join the Army of the Confederacy. Now, however, the fort was a crumbling relic. Most of the cut stones and rocks had been carted away to be used to construct the schoolhouse. There were still, however, several structures standing—the quarters of the married officers, he had been told. It looked like a good place to run into a nest of rattlesnakes.

Then he was into the town, coming into the square from the east side. The undertaker's parlor was at the far northwest corner, catty-corner from the jail. As he rode along, leading the horse carrying Horne's body, the townspeople came out of their shops and homes to watch his passage. Several called out, inquiring who his load was, but he paid them no mind. It was his conviction that most people had way too much interest in things, especially when it comes to things that were none of their business.

He rode into the alley behind the undertaker's, left his horses, and pounded on the back door. When a man came, Longarm indicated the body and directed that the body be taken in. The undertaker himself came out, and Longarm gave him instructions about getting a photographer and having a tintype of the man's face made. He said, "And I don't want him buried for twenty-four hours. But get him ready for viewing, as I am liable to be bringing some folks by to make an identification." He gave the undertaker ten dollars to get him started, got a receipt, and mounted up and rode over to the sheriff's office.

He had expected to fetch Bodenheimer, walk him over to the undertaker's, see what he had to say about Gus Horne, and then head on back for Hannah's cabin. But to his agitation and irritation, the office was full of a mayor and three city councilmen, all of whom were in an indignant mood.

They came crowding at him the moment he entered the door. A short, plump man in a swallowtail coat and vest with, incongruously, a derby hat was in the forefront, shaking a plump forefinger at Longarm. He said, "Now you look here, Marshal, I am Bower Arp and I am the mayor of this town, and I am ordering you right now to release our sheriff and his deputies."

Longarm pushed the forefinger away with some annoyance. He said, "Well, Mayor Arp, you can order all you want to, but it ain't going to do you a bit of good."

That started the three councilmen yelling. They were not as well turned out as the mayor, but they were no less vocal. Longarm finally shouted, *"Shut up!"*

He glanced over at Melvin Purliss, who was standing

by looking helpless. Then he looked back at his tormentors. He said to the mayor, "Now Mayor Arp, let's me and you get one thing straight. Bodenheimer and his deputies are not yours. They are county law officers. They can operate inside your town, but they are elected officials, at least Bodenheimer is, who only answer to county government. The only law you can have in a town is a marshal or a police force. Now, do I have either one of them locked up? Huh? Tell me."

The mayor began to bluster, but it did him no good. Finally he said, "You are leaving us with no law, Marshal. You'll be gone and we'll have no law to protect us."

Longarm gave him a hard look. "Then why don't you appoint you a town marshal or a police chief?"

The little fat man worked his mouth a few times and finally managed a weak, "Well, I don't know. It never seemed necessary before. Besides, who'd want the job."

"Yeah," Longarm said dryly, "it might dry up a major source of income for the town."

The mayor gave him a look. "I do not know what you are talking about, sir."

Longarm nodded. "I'll just bet you don't, Mayor. Now, I tell you what. You and your boys get the hell on out of this jail and don't come back. You do, I'm more than likely going to arrest and jail you for interfering with a federal officer in the performance of his duty."

The mayor's mouth worked again as the rage rose in him. He said, "By damn, sir! By damn! There will be more than one telegram sent to your superiors before this day is much older. You can depend on that! By damn, you do not know who you are dealing with, sir!"

"Oh, yeah, I do. I figure a telegram from you would be the same as a step up in my career."

The mayor got red in the face. He shook his finger again. "Damn you, sir! I am not only the mayor, I am also the town dentist. You will rue the day you get a toothache in this town!''

With that he gathered his dignity around him and marched out, leading his small pack of councilmen out onto the street. Longarm closed the door behind them and then turned to Purliss. ''Well, Deputy, how are the prisoners?''

But Purliss said reproachfully, ''Marshal, you right shore you ought to have talked to the mayor like that? He do be the boss, you know.''

Longarm stared at him in amazement. ''Where did you get that idea? Didn't you just hear what I told him? He comes back in this jail you chunk him out on his ear. And I don't want Bodenheimer having any visitors, even his wife.''

''But the mayor is supposed to be the boss of the town, ain't that right? Ain't he like the foreman?''

''Listen, Purliss, you are a county deputy. You are standing on county property. Get the mayor out of your mind. Now, I want you to bring Bodenheimer out here. I'm going to take him over to the undertaker's.''

''The where?''

Longarm stared at him. ''Melvin, you are starting to irritate me. Won't take much more and you'll be jailing yourself. Now get Bodenheimer. None of the others, just him.''

When Purliss brought Bodenheimer out into the office, Longarm was not surprised to see the man looking duller than ever. But now his clothes were rumpled and he needed a shave. He said immediately, ''You come to turn us loose?''

''No. There's a dead man over at the undertaker's. I'm going to take you over there to look at him. If you can tell me anything about him it will help your case with me.''

Bodenheimer stared back. ''I ain't got to go nowhere with you.''

"That's right," Longarm said evenly. "And I don't have to feed you or give you water. How will you have it?"

Bodenheimer said matter-of-factly, "I'll get you one of these days."

But he agreed to come along. They went out on the street. Longarm had not bothered to manacle the man or hold a pistol on him. As they walked across the street people stopped and pointed and whispered to each other. Longarm had no doubt that the word had spread throughout the area that the sheriff had been arrested.

Inside the undertaker's parlor they looked down at the man Longarm knew as Gus Horne. He was laid out on a wooden bench. Bodenheimer barely gave him a glance. "Don't know him."

"You've never seen this man?"

"Not until now."

"He married Dalton Diver's daughter less than six weeks ago. Hannah."

"Wasn't at the wedding."

"This your last word on the subject, Bodenheimer?"

"Yep."

"Then that is one more mark against you. I think you are lying. No, I know you are lying."

"You better let me out of that jail or you are going to be in a hell of a lot of trouble."

"Turn around and get out that door. You're going back. This fresh air just causes you to lie better."

He was very conscious of the time and very conscious that he had promised Hannah to be back in a hurry. It was, he calculated, pushing two o'clock. But he was hungry. It had been a long time since breakfast, and he went to the hotel dining room to see if they wouldn't fix him something quick. The dining room was closed, but Longarm talked the desk clerk into getting the cook to fry him up some potatoes and a steak. He got a beer out of the bar and then dined in solitude, very aware that Hannah was probably starting to fume. But what the hell, he thought, she'd waited this long, one more hour wasn't going to hurt.

He paid his score, leaving an extra dollar for the cook, and then sauntered out of the hotel. He was about to mount up when he saw a horseman coming at a lope down a street from the west. Longarm paused and watched. Soon it became clear that the man was Austin Davis. Longarm stood there, the reins in his hand, waiting. In another moment Davis was reining in at the front of the hotel. He dismounted and said, "Longarm, we need to have a talk."

"It will have to wait. I got a hot young virgin ready to come out of the oven. She's probably already mad as hell."

Davis looked agitated. "No, that will have to wait. Let's go in your room and take a drink. Hell, I need a drink. Something happened."

Longarm led the way through the lobby and down the hall to his room. He unlocked the door, and they took seats at the table as they had the night before. Longarm said, "Now what's this all about?"

Davis took his hat off and ran his hand through his hair. He said, "You was more than right what you said about me making an enemy. Amos Goustwhite had it in his mind, not a half an hour ago, to blow my head off."

"What happened?"

"I was cutting cross-country, coming back from that Rebeccah's, when Goustwhite stepped out of a wild plum thicket with about a ten-bore double-barreled shotgun pointing right at me. Wasn't ten yards away. Only thing that saved me was he seemed like he wanted to say something before he fired—something to make me sorry for what I done to him, I reckon."

"And you weren't in the mood for conversation."

"See how much you feel like talking when some idiot

is setting up to cut you in half. I wheeled my horse sideways, drawing my revolver, and leaned under my horse's neck and put two in his chest.''

"He ever fire the scattergun?"

"Yeah, but by that time he was going over backwards. All he could have done was shot down any ducks might have been flying over.''

"He dead?"

Davis reached out, poured himself a drink, and downed it before he answered. "If he hadn't of been, you wouldn't be seeing me.''

"Where's the body?"

"Laying right where I left it. Or where he left it. Or where my slugs left it. His horse was tied inside the thicket of plum trees. Was pretty dense in there.''

"How you figure he knew where to lay for you?"

Davis gave a brief laugh. "That's easy. My big mouth. After breakfast I went into the saloon and went to asking directions of this Rebeccah's place. Said I was a friend of her husband's and had word for her. I got the directions, all right, but I also got more than I bargained for. I figure some friend of Goustwhite's got word to him. Longarm, I tell you the truth. It does not do my nerves one bit of good to have some sonofabitch point a double-barreled shotgun at me at such a range. Them damn things will blow you to pieces. If the bastard had stayed under cover and just fired as I rode by, you would be mourning at my gravesite.''

Longarm said dryly, "I doubt there'd have been that much of you to bury. I thought you broke the bastard's arm.''

"His forearm. He had a splint on it and bandages, but it didn't hinder him none with that big shotgun. You ain't got to be accurate with one of them damn things, just close. And he was as close as I ever want anybody to get. Unless she is a naked girl. Now I wish I'd broke both his arms.''

"What about his horse?"

"I left him tied. The place ain't a mile out of town. I wanted to see you and figure out what you wanted to do before I went off on my own."

"I wasn't supposed to be in town."

Davis nodded. "I know it. You were headed out for that Hannah girl's place. But I didn't know where it was, so I come to get directions. And then I seen you in front of the hotel."

Longarm thought of the interruption he'd had the day before. He said, "So you was planning on riding up to her cabin and banging on the door just to tell me you'd shot Goustwhite? No matter what you reckoned I'd be doing inside?"

Davis gave him a slight smile. "Hell, Longarm, anybody knows law work is hard work. Your duty comes first."

"So the horse and the body are still there."

"Yeah," Davis said, "but I went through his pockets and his saddlebags first." He went to digging in the pockets of his riding pants. "Made quite a little haul. Man was doing uncommonly well for a saloon tough. He had two hundred dollars in paper cash and gold in his saddlebags and eighty dollars in his pocket." He put it on the table in a crumpled ball. "Seems like quite a wad for a poker player of his caliber to be carrying. He also had this." Davis reached in his pocket and came out with a piece of folded paper. He opened it. "Where you reckon he got that?"

It was a check, made out to the County Line Auction Barn and signed by some cattleman Longarm didn't know. The amount was $190. Longarm said, "Well, this tells us where he got the cash. I'd have to reckon he was one of the robbers."

Davis shook his head. "That is the damnedest thing I ever heard of. Is the whole damn county crooked? What in hell is going on here?"

Longarm looked thoughtfully across the room for a moment. Then he sighed and said, "I don't know. But I think it is going to be hard as hell to prove up. I once chased a gang run by a family name of the Gallaghers. They roved back and forth across New Mexico, but mainly headquartered in Oklahoma Territory and Arkansas. If you got close to them they'd just kind of disappear and turn up as ranch hands and farm hands and even storekeepers. But that was over one hell of a big territory, and when they got the gang together they'd stay together for months at a time. This bunch looks like they gather up, pull a job, and head for the house before supper."

"Can you think of a loose end you might could get hold of and we could pull and unravel the whole thing?"

Longarm shook his head. "Right now I ain't got an idea. But you wasn't the only one had a little excitement this morning." He shoved his hand in his pocket and came out with the money and the checks he'd taken off Gus Horne. He piled it all on top of the table with what Davis had brought.

Davis's mouth dropped open. "Where in hell did you get that?"

"Just about the same place you did." In a few words he described what had happened on his way to Hannah's. He finished and said, "I guess we know who two members of that gang were. Too bad they are dead and can't tell us who else was with them."

Davis whistled slowly. "I'd say we come off on the lucky end. If your man don't tie his horse so close that your horse shies, then odds are he don't hit your saddlehorn, but a big piece of *you*. And if ol' Amos hadn't felt the need to tell me why he was fixing to blow me to smithereens, I would have been blown to smithereens. Hell, Longarm, I think we are in the kingdom of the bushwhackers."

Longarm said, "I believe that was my advice to you

before you set out to court Rebeccah." He picked at the money and checks. "Must be nearly a thousand dollars here."

"What are you going to do with it?"

"Take it out to the auction barn and give it to Ownsby. It's his money. By the way, how did you get on with Rebeccah?"

Austin Davis slumped back in his chair and looked up at the ceiling. "That was something I meant to mention. Marshal, we was going great guns there at first. She was giving me every signal a woman can give a man. And say, she ain't bad-looking at all. I damn shore wouldn't throw rocks at her."

"You get a hand on her?"

"Near about. We was both sitting on the same divan and she had a leg up so I could see some thigh. But then . . ." Austin Davis slapped his thigh. "Then I taken it into my head, heavens knows why, to bring up Vince Diver. I said I'd known him down along the border and in other places and the name was unusual, and I wondered if they might be kin."

"What happened?"

Davis slapped the top of the table with the flat of his hand. "Nothing happened, that's what. I might as well have shoved a chunk of ice up her glory hole. The minute I mentioned that name the fun was over. She done everything but ask me to leave."

Longarm mulled it over a moment. "You must have struck a nerve. But you are still going to have to go back out there and work your way back in."

"How?"

Longarm got up. "I don't know right now. But time is a-wasting and I want you to get a look at this Gus Horne I shot. See if you've ever come across him in your travels."

As they walked from the hotel to the undertaker's,

Longarm said, "Austin, you can't tell anybody that you killed Amos Goustwhite."

Davis looked at him. "Why not?"

"Because he is part of the town. He's got kin here. Like you said, this may be the kingdom of the bush-whackers. These people are pretty close-knit. No, that's one you can't claim."

"But what if there is paper out on him?"

Longarm gave him a disgusted look. "Hell, he's a town rowdy. Ain't no paper out on him. He's a home-grown outlaw. You figure Bodenheimer has put out wanted notices on him? Hell, besides, you're making three dollars a day. What do you want?"

"Then who is supposed to have killed him?"

"I reckon me."

Davis stopped. They were in front of a dry goods store. "And I suppose you can't be bushwhacked."

"Folks think a minute or two more about backshoot-ing a federal marshal than they do a tinhorn gambler."

"Tinhorn—hey, wait just a damn minute."

But Longarm was walking on. By the time Austin Davis had caught up they were turning into the under-taking parlor. Hatcher, the undertaker, came bustling for-ward to meet them. He was a short, balding man in a shabby suit who looked glad for the business. He said, "Yessir, Marshal. Can I he'p you?"

"We need to have another look at that body. Gus Horne."

"Yessir, yessir. If you'll just step right this way. By the way, Marshal, the photographer has been in and the picture was taken just as you asked."

Davis said, "For your scrapbook, Marshal?"

Longarm gave him a sour look. "I can't believe somebody ain't killed you before now, Davis. Now take a look at Gus Horne here and see if you know him."

Chapter 6

Austin Davis looked down at the dead face. He said, "Hell, this here is Gus White."

"You sure?" The name matched the initials G.W.

"Hell, yes. I've knowed him in different places down along the border for the last three or four years. Say he was calling himself Horne, Gus Horne?"

"Yeah."

Davis shrugged. "That might have been his right name, but I knew him as Gus White. Course some of them fellers changed their names 'bout as often as they changed their shirts. Last I heard of him he was doing a little time in the state prison in Huntsville."

Longarm stared at the face, calculating. "What did he get up to?"

Davis said, "You understand I never knowed him all that well except to see around the saloon or run up against in a poker game. But he got up to what most of them did. Robbery, cattle rustling, dealing in stolen cattle, smuggling a little gold. Might have been in a shooting scrape or two, I couldn't say. I wonder what in hell brought him here."

Longarm said, "Yeah, me too." He turned to the undertaker. "Well, much obliged, Mister Hatcher. You can plant him anytime you're of a mind."

He took Austin Davis by the shoulder and steered him to the door and out onto the street. Davis said, "What the hell's the hurry?"

"I didn't want you saying anything about Goustwhite. I don't think we'll be bringing him in."

Austin Davis looked at him. "What is going on now?"

Longarm frowned. "Say you was going into a business and you didn't know much about how to run it. What would you do?"

Davis thought a moment. "Well, I reckon I'd fetch me in somebody who did. Bring in some outside help. Why?"

Longarm said slowly, "That's what I been kind of thinking. I reckon somebody here decided to start a new business, but didn't figure he had the know-how for it. So he sent for outside help. Like Gus Horne. Or White, or whatever his name was. There's been several others killed. Near as I can find out, they ain't boys from this town or this county." He stopped and stared across the street at the courthouse. "Austin, we may have just run across the damnedest operation I ever had a hand in." Then he turned abruptly to Davis. "Listen, I don't want the home folks to know Goustwhite has been killed. Hell, I don't know how deep this thing goes. Might be everybody in town is part of it. You ride back out there and hide that body. Roll it into a ravine or something. Stuff it up in a thicket, but get it well hid. Ground up there is too hard to dig a hole."

"What about his horse?"

"Take the bridle and saddle off and turn him loose. You might see which way he heads if he takes it into his head to home."

"And Rebeccah?"

"Go on back there. Get in on some excuse. Tell her you lost your wallet. And don't mention Vince Diver again. Hell, you claim to be a hand with the ladies. Well, prove it. And for heaven's sake, don't let nobody know you killed Goustwhite. That could be fatal.''

"Where you going?"

Longarm sighed. "I'm going out to visit Miss Hannah. And you can believe it or not, but I ain't looking forward to it. And she is as pretty a piece of quail as I've laid my eyes on in some time."

"What about that money and them checks?"

Longarm had gotten a large envelope from the desk clerk and put the cash and checks in it. He'd sealed it and had the clerk put it in the hotel safe. He sighed and said, "I'd like to have gotten it to the Ownsbys today, but I just don't have the time. Tomorrow will be soon enough, I reckon. I fear for my life from Miss Hannah as it is. I swore to her I'd be back within the hour. What time is it? Hell, it's heading for four o'clock. She is going to tear me limb from limb.''

Davis said dryly, "You sure you ain't kind of putting on the dog? I mean, I been here four days and it appears you can walk down the street without having the female population make a churning charge at you.''

Longarm gave him a pained expression. "It ain't that it's me. It's me that she has fastened on to to show her the mysteries of what she's been guessing about all her life. It should have happened yesterday, but the sheriff interrupted that.''

"What about that sheriff? You going to be able to keep him jailed? I can't believe, if this town is as crooked as you think it is, that somebody or other ain't going to break him out. I don't think they want you running around here loose.''

Longarm turned his head toward Davis so he could look him in the eye. "Which means we had better get to smoking. Don't ask Rebeccah no more leading questions. Stay away from the bandit business. See if you can find out what it would take to win her hand.''

Davis looked startled. "Now just a damn minute. I ain't got no interest in getting married."

"I didn't say you had to actually marry her. See if she'll put a figure on her bride price. Hell, work her a little. Pretend you are actually a good poker player and play her like you would a hand of cards. Act like you had good sense."

Davis turned and started for his horse. He said, "I wouldn't be going around talking about having good sense. Somebody is liable to ask you to trot yours out and show it."

He stopped Hannah's angry petulance by simply walking in the door and taking off her clothes. There were not that many to take off. All she was wearing was a blue cotton frock and a little shirtwaist with a slip on underneath. At first she had started to protest, but by the time he had her standing by the bed, pink and glowing and starting to tremble, her mouth was shut except for the quickened breathing that came through her slightly parted lips.

He stepped close to her and kissed her, only having to gently remind her with his tongue for her to open her mouth. After that she kissed him wetly and hungrily, probing with her own tongue and pressing her softness against him. Finally he took his mouth away from hers and began kissing her neck and ear and then her shoulders. Her breath was coming faster and faster. He dropped to his knees. Her breasts were just on a height even with his mouth. He took her nipples, one by one, into his mouth, putting his arms around her, caressing her smooth, firm buttocks. Now she was trembling and gasping. It was cool in the cabin, but her nipples and rosettes were much harder and more crinkled than just from the cold. He kissed the underside of her breasts, licking them, and then worked his way down her stomach to the very edge of the light brown, silky bush that

93

flared up from the fat little mound that always reminded him of a quail breast.

She was rocking back and forth, tearing at his hair. She said, between gasps, "I want to . . . to see you. Take . . . off . . . your . . . clothes!"

He stood up and sat down on the side of the bed and ripped his boots off. Then he shucked his shirt and slipped down his jeans until they all lay on a pile on the floor. He stood up. Her eyes immediately went to his penis. Her eyes got round. She said, "Ooooh, it's so big! Is that going in me?"

"Yes."

She put out her hand. "Can I touch it?"

"All you want."

For a moment she held it in both her soft little hands, moving it, feeling how stiff it was. Then hesitantly, she found his testicles and cradled them in her hands. He was having to grit his teeth. Her touch was as light as the end of a feather.

Finally, when he could stand it no longer, he took her by the shoulders and laid her across the bed, opening her legs wide. He lay down partly on top of her so that he could kiss her breasts and then her stomach and then the inside of her thighs. She instinctively pulled her knees up, exposing herself more readily to his mouth. He worked his way through the silken hairs until he found her clitoris buried in the wet, warm, pink flesh. As soon as his tongue touched it, she let out a little cry and arched her back. She said, "Eiiiiii! Ooooh! What's that? What are you doing?"

He took her hand and guided it to the little bump and explained to her what it was. She said, between gasps, "Ohhhh, do that some more! Do it! Do it!"

He lowered his head, and was about to search for her clitoris with his tongue when she suddenly seized him by the head with both her hands, pulling his face deep into her warm, young vagina. As he found her clitoris, she began to rhythmically pump her hips against him, gradually raising her buttocks off the bed, arching her back, pumping faster and faster. In less than a moment she let out a high, keening cry and stayed frozen at the top of her arch, her hands pulling at his hair, her cry going higher and higher and louder and louder.

Then she suddenly collapsed. She lay still for a moment, her breathing heavy and hard. Gradually it slowed. He lay still, letting her savor the feeling. After a moment she said, "Oh, my. Oh, my. Oh, that was wonderful."

He said, "It's supposed to be."

She found his arm with her hand and tugged him upward. She said, "I want to taste you. Come up here and let me see."

He got up and knee-walked on the bed until he was in front of her face. He leaned down slightly as she raised up on one elbow. He was going to guide it into her mouth, but she suddenly darted forward with her lips parted and enveloped him. It amazed him how deep she could take him. But he had only a second to be amazed as she began to slide her lips back and forth and to work her tongue. He was gritting his teeth, holding on.

Finally he pulled away from her and turned her on her back and lay on top of her, kissing her mouth while he brought himself under control. Finally he spread her legs with his and then made a forward thrust. It went deep inside her. She was so wet and so open that his penis did not have to be guided.

She said, "Oooooh!" and arched her back and threw her arms around his neck, pulling his mouth to hers. With his hands he reached back and lifted her legs, showing her how to put them up and lock them around him.

As he began to move in and out of her, her breath began blowing louder and louder in his ear. He moved his body slightly so he could be sure his penis was sliding across her clitoris. As he made contact with her, she began to move faster and faster, her hands leaving his neck and clawing at his back. Her legs were so tight around his waist he thought she was going to squeeze him in two. She rose and fell, rose and fell with him. He could feel, by the heat of her body, that she was coming up, coming up, coming up higher and higher.

And then that foggy cloud drifted down behind his eyes as it always did, and all he was aware of was the feel of her, inside and out, and the sensations that were running through his body. And then he started climbing up that steep cliff. He went up and up and up, and then there was an explosion and he could feel himself falling. He fell for a long time. Falling slower and slower and slower. At long last he came to rest lying on top of her.

"Aaaaah," he said. He could feel the sweat between them, even in the cool room. With a sigh he slipped off her and flopped over on his back on the mattress. "Ooooh, me," he said. His arms and legs felt like they were made out of lead.

She put her hand on his chest and ran her fingers through the curly hair, then said in a little voice, "That was ever so nice. Let's do it some more."

He laughed in spite of himself and said, "Hannah, honey, it ain't like that for a man. He needs a little time to rest in between."

She reached down and found his member. She said, "My goodness. What happened to this? It ain't half the size it was."

She really was an innocent. When she hadn't bled he'd wondered if she really was a virgin, but girls who rode horses generally broke their maidenheads long before they were old enough to learn about sex. He said, "That's what I'm talking about. A man has to rest. You wore it down to a nub. It's got to grow back."

"Is that right?" She sounded alarmed.

He laughed and sat up. He wanted a smoke and a drink of whiskey. Over her strong protests he tried to put on his socks so he could pull on his boots. She said, "Don't get up yet, Marshal. Let's do it again."

He shook his head. "Hannah, honey, a man ain't like that. It takes a while."

"Well, when?"

He glanced at the window and saw twilight descending. He said, "You owe me supper. After I eat."

"How come we can't before then?"

He pulled on a boot. "Hannah, when a man drops his load it takes him a while to build it back up. It's like the opposite of eating a big meal. You ain't hungry right away. It takes a little time." He looked around at her, admiring the shape and symmetry of her body. "A woman is lucky that way. And you are luckier than most."

"How am I luckier?"

He said, "You've got a big and a prominent clitoris. It's easy for my big old dong to work back and forth on it. That's what makes you climax."

"What's that?"

It made him smile because it had been so long since he had instructed a woman about her body. He reached in and felt around until he could touch the now-soft clitoris up at the top of her vagina. He said, "You know how you go up and up and up and then you kind of explode inside?"

She put her hand on his and moved her hips against his finger. "You mean when it feels good all over?"

"When you yell. When you scream."

"Did I scream?"

"Several times. Well, that's the climax. But you can do it more than one time. In fact, I think you did it about four times."

"But how am I luckier?" She now had his hand gripped with both of hers. With an effort he pulled it back from between her legs.

He said, "Because most women's clitoris is kind of

buried down deep and the man's member doesn't touch it. Sometimes it's way up and out of position. Then those women, unless the man knows what to do with his tongue and his finger, don't ever have a climax.''

"How come you know so much?"

He pulled up his jeans and then put on his boots. He stood up. "You better get up, girl, and see about fixing me some supper. I ain't going to answer any more questions until I get fed.''

She made him a supper of steak and mashed potatoes and gravy with canned tomatoes. She didn't eat, but sat across from him with her elbows propped on the table and her face in her hands, staring at him. He had had a difficult time getting her to put on some clothes. She had set out to fix the supper in her bare skin, but he had explained that was too hard on him. He'd said, "Hannah, you go around like that, you are going to get me all heated up for no purpose. And then I'll be like a piece of meat you keep heating and not eating and then warming up again. Pretty soon I'll get so tough and tasteless you won't want no part of me." In the end she had consented to put on a thin, cotton wrapper that went around once and then tied with a sash. But the sash kept coming undone, and besides, the wrapper wasn't up to the job it was intended for. Her breasts kept falling out, or the bottom part of the wrapper would open clear to her downy bush. It was, Longarm thought, about like trying to hide a horse under a hankerchief.

She watched him, never taking her eyes off his face. She said, "How come you know so much about, about . . .'' She made a gesture toward the bed. "About all that stuff?''

He said, "Same way I know about horses and guns. I've had the use of them.''

"You mean you've done it a lot.''

He smiled. "Well, not as much as I've wanted to. But

I reckon every man can say that."

She made a pouty face. "I wish I was experienced like you."

He put his fork down. "Oh, no, you don't." He glanced off into the distance, remembering. "I wish, just once, I could go back to when it was all brand-new." He shook his head. "Enjoy this part, girl. It won't ever be like this again."

"You mean you get tired of it?"

"No, not if you're normal. I guess maybe a woman might. But I ain't ever going to get worn out with it." He smiled. "Though I'd like to die trying. No, it's just that the first few times are special. Kind of like opening up a present that's all wrapped in bright paper and ribbon. You don't want to rush it."

When he was finished eating, he poured himself a glass of whiskey and lit a cigar. When he had gone out to get the bottle of whiskey, he had unsaddled and taken the bridle off his horse and turned him into the little catch pen behind Hannah's cabin where he knew there was feed and water. He had no plans to spend the night, but he figured he might be quite late, and he had not wanted his horse to stand tied for several hours.

He looked at Hannah through the cloud of blue smoke, wondering just how much she knew. She did a good job of playing a simple half-woman, half-girl, but he wondered if it was all true. He knew that women married men back in the woods without ever really knowing the men, but it appeared that Dalton Diver had brought the practice to a fine art. He said, "Hannah, when I rode up with Gus Horne's body, you never so much as turned a hair. He was your husband. Didn't you feel anything?"

She gave a half shrug. "I never knowed the man. Never so much as touched him. Why should I feel sad 'bout somebody I didn't know? Hell, I never felt like he was my husband. I never even got piece of paper that said so. Daddy's got it, I reckon.''

"Well how did you meet this man, this Gus Horne?"

She shrugged again. She said vaguely, "I don't know. He just showed up out at Daddy's place. There was still about five or six of us girls still living there, and he just kind of walked around and looked things over. Then he and Daddy went in his office and I guess they talked and whatnot. What are you askin' me all these questions for?"

Longarm gave her a disarming smile. "Because I'm a federal marshal, honey, and they don't pay me if I don't ask questions."

She reached across the table and slapped his hand. "Oh, you silly. Let's not be talkin' 'bout these old things. Why don't we get in bed. Startin' to get all nippy in here."

He laughed. "I reckon it could be summertime and you'd still say it was nippy. Listen now, you don't want to rush a good thing. Let's let the pot stew a little while. I kind of find it hard to believe that four of you married members of that gang."

"Well, hell, like Daddy said, they was the only ones had the money, or the way to get it. Listen, you ought not to be talkin' bad 'bout that bunch. Daddy says the county is mighty grateful to them. They go outside and bring money back, money that is sore needed around here. Nosir, I ain't ashamed of marryin' Gus Horne. What I'm ashamed of was he left me a widder woman without no marriage-bed ceremonies. A girl ought not to have to go lookin' on her own, especially when she'd done already got herself a husband."

Longarm said patiently, "You told me once that Lester Gaskamp was supposed to be a Mason County boy. Did you know him before?"

"Before he married Rebeccah? Before he went to robbing and banditry?" She pulled a face. "Tell you the truth, Marshal, I never set eyes on the man. I'm just goin' on what I was told. He might have been from the moon for all I know."

"Four of y'all married into the gang."

She furrowed her brow. "Well, I'm not all that sure about that. Could have been my sister Rachel got her one too. She married right after Rebeccah, but she moved off. Clear to Rock Springs. And that's a good piece away."

"What makes you think he might have been an outlaw?"

She made a motion in the air with her hands. "I don't know. About six months ago he come to the house—that was when I was still livin' with Daddy. And he was just bristlin' with pistols. Him and Daddy talked, and then Daddy said he wanted to show me somethin'. So me and Daddy got in the buggy, and this man followed us on his horse, and we come down here."

"Here where?"

"Here. Right here. Right to this house. This cabin. Of course it belonged to Ol' Man Summers then. He was a old man who'd moved down here a couple of years ago after his wife died."

"What then?"

She pulled a face. "Then nothin'. Daddy asked me how I liked the place and I said fine. Then we went on back to Daddy's house. Wasn't that much longer till Ol' Man Summers died. Must have fallen in the river an' drowned. Didn't find his body for a month. It had washed down the river clear to Llano, nearly."

"What was the name of Rachel's husband?"

She frowned and bit at her lower lip. "What was that boy's name?" She frowned harder, furrowing her brow. "Well, Dan was his first name. I know the other. It was the same as some folks used to live here but they moved away. He wasn't no kin to them, though. Laws, I got it right here on the tip of my tongue." As if to illustrate, she ran the pink thing around her lips. The sight caused a stirring in Longarm's crotch, but he quelled it. He had heard her very distinctly when she had talked about the old man named Summers who so conveniently drowned after she told her daddy she liked his place. He had not said anything because he was far more interested in this man she was talking about, this husband of Rachel's, the man just "bristling with pistols" and living in Rock Springs, the town where Austin Davis had said he'd run across a man named Vince Diver.

"Hicks, it was!" she said triumphantly. "I knowed I'd get it. Momma always said I was smart as paint and argued with Daddy about marrying me to any outlaw."

"But she didn't get her way."

Hannah made a swipe at her hair. "Huh, Momma always got her way. Daddy told her the first marriage didn't count. That was just to help the family out. He told her not to worry, he'd see me right in the husband department. Say, you ain't married, are you?"

He smiled. "We done been through that, Hannah. The law doesn't allow a federal officer to get married on account of his work."

"Oh, yeah, that's right. I don't reckon it makes no difference. Daddy says my second husband is going to have to have a pile of money." She blew a strand of hair away from her face. "And now that you are helping educate me in bed, I'll make somebody a fine wife. Maybe marry a banker or a lawyer or a senator or something."

He sat, sipping at his whiskey and admiring what he could see of her across the table. The wrapper had fallen open, and her fresh, firm breasts were revealed to the strawberry-sized nipples. Someday they would be sagging and old, but now they were so firm and erect you could see the rounded bottoms of each. Longarm was a connossieur of women's breasts, and he was hard pressed to remember when he'd seen a pair to match Hannah's in perfection and symmetry. He was also trying to think of some way to probe her about the men who had come to her father's place without making her suspicious. He said, "Hannah, you talked about Dan Hicks, Rachel's husband, showing up. Weren't you at the wedding?"

"Naw. One morning Daddy loaded her up in a buggy and they drove off. Daddy came back two days later without her. She wrote and said she was married and just happy as a lark."

"Do a lot of men come around your daddy's place?"

"Well, laws, yes. Daddy's in politics, don't you know, and they got to come out and talk to him over a jug of whiskey."

"What do you mean your daddy is in politics?"

She looked prim. "Well, he says who gets to be representative and go up to Austin. And I think senator too. Though I ain't real sure about that. And the mayor and the sheriff. Why, even the banker comes out to talk to him. My daddy is mighty important."

"What about this place?" He raised his hand and made a circle to include the cabin. "Didn't you think it was kind of odd Mister Summers dying right when he did? I mean, you were going to marry Gus Horne and he needed a place. I bet he got it cheap. What'd you think?"

She shrugged. "Why, I never thought nothing at all about it. Daddy says we all got to go sometime and that old man was being foolish living this close to a river. Daddy says the river most likely got on a rise and swept him plumb away." She suddenly frowned. "But how come we are talking about all this? I thought you was gonna tell me about your first time. And when are we gonna get back in bed?"

He held up his glass, which still contained about an inch of whiskey. "Let me finish this first. Hell, girl, I got to rest. I'm the one doing most of the work. By the way, how old is your daddy?"

"Daddy?" The question caught her off guard, and for a second her face was blank. Then she frowned. "Oh, he's old. I'd guess he's fifty. Somewheres in there. Why?"

"No reason." He took a sip of his whiskey. "And there's just you girls. Ten of you?"

"That's right. Daddy says he should have worn his boots to bed. That's the way you get boys."

He said, making his voice casual, "Funny thing. Not too long back, I run into a Vince Diver. Wondered if he might be some kin of yours."

He was watching her eyes. For a second he saw a furtive shrinking of her pupils, but then it passed and her face went back to its open and innocent self. She said, shaking her head, "No relation that I know of."

"It ain't exactly a common name."

She shrugged. "I wouldn't know. I never even been out of the county. No, I take that back. Daddy took us all to Llano for the fair one time. Ain't you through with that whiskey yet?"

He had not meant to spend the night, but Hannah was so demanding and voracious that he finally fell asleep during one of the few times she let him rest. He awoke with the weak light of the false dawn leaking through the windows and Hannah curled up in a ball next to him, sound asleep. He eased out of bed as quietly as he could, gathered up his clothes and his boots and his gunbelt, and stole silently out the door of the cabin, closing it quietly behind him. As a general rule he was a morning man when it came to a little fun, but he didn't have anything left and the last thing he wanted to do was fight Hannah off.

He dressed standing out in the cold dimness, shivering as he buttoned up his shirt and then got his jeans and socks on. He pulled on his boots, strapped his gunbelt in place, and then stole quietly around the cabin and got his horse saddled and bridled. The horse wanted to nicker at him, but he covered the horse's nose with his hand and led him out of the pen and about twenty yards up the path before he mounted. When he had a mile between himself and the cabin he let out a breath and shook his head. Never in his life could he have figured on some little slip of a girl doing him down and causing him to cry Uncle, but that was damn near what had happened.

As he approached town he wondered about Austin Davis and how he had made out. But the first thing he wanted was some breakfast and then maybe a nap. He didn't know what time he had finally fallen asleep, but he knew it was late. He rode straight to the hotel and put his horse in the livery, and then walked around to the front and passed through the lobby on his way to the dining room. As soon as he stepped into the lobby Austin Davis got up and came to him. "I got to talk to you," Davis said.

"Let's eat some breakfast."

"I already ate, but I'll drink a cup of coffee. Something has happened and I don't know what to make of it."

They were going into the dining room. Longarm sat down at the first empty table he saw. He said, "Let me get some food in me and then fire away. What are you doing in town? Didn't you see Rebeccah?"

"Yeah, and I need to talk about that with you. But that ain't all."

They didn't speak again until Longarm had put away a half-dozen fried eggs, a ham steak, and half-a-dozen biscuits. When he was through he wiped his mouth on his napkin and said, "Now. What's the big news."

"Well," Austin Davis said, "for openers, Amos Goustwhite's body is gone."

"What do you mean, gone?"

"I mean up and disappeared. Horse too."

Longarm stared at him, not sure what the information meant. "Did you find sign where the body might have been dragged off? Or were there wagon tracks or anything?"

Davis shook his head. "Nope. Nothing. Of course that country is so damn hard and rocky, but there should have been some kind of sign. But I didn't see any indication that a party had been in there. There was horse tracks, of course, and boot marks, but they could have been mine. You can't figure time on sign in that hard a ground. Best I could say was that somebody come along, loaded Goustwhite across his horse, and rode off with him."

"You check the undertaker?"

Davis nodded. "Right before you come in. He was just up. But no, there wasn't no fresh bodies. I couldn't just up and ask about Goustwhite because I'm the only one supposed to know he's dead."

"Hmmmmm." Longarm rubbed his beard. He wanted a shave, but it was coming very close to decision time on a number of matters. He said, "You get anything out of Rebeccah?"

Austin shook his head. "Not anywhere near what I put in her, I'll tell you that. That woman is a bottomless pit. I couldn't fill her up fast enough. If I hadn't been on duty, I'd of thought I was having a pretty good time until about the fourth go-around."

"It must run in the family," Longarm said. He told Davis a little about his evening. "You didn't stay the night, did you?"

Davis shook his head. "She played out about midnight and I struck a trot out of there. I needed a rest. Besides, I was anxious to tell you about Goustwhite disappearing."

Longarm said, "Does the name Dan Hicks mean anything to you?"

Davis looked startled. "Where the hell did you hear that name?"

Longarm told him. "What about it?"

Davis pushed his hat back. "Hell, Longarm, he used to be a running mate of that Vince Diver we been talking about. But I thought Hicks was doing some state prison time up in Huntsville."

Longarm got up. "Let's go to my room. I'm just about filled plumb up with this foolishness. Somebody is playing fast and loose with the law and I intend on putting a stop to it. We got to sit down and lay our cards out and see what kind of hand we got."

"You sure you don't want me to go back out there and question that Rebeccah again? I've nearly recovered."

Longarm gave him a look as they walked out of the dining room. "Why don't you try and act like a law officer even if you ain't got the makings of one."

Davis said, "By the way. I didn't mention it, but that Rebeccah woman has a damn fine house with good furniture. Two-story. And she's got some good horses and some mighty fat beef cattle that are kept up in a feed lot."

Longarm said, "I ain't surprised, the money they are taking in."

"But her husband is dead."

Longarm gave him a look. "Maybe he is and maybe he ain't. I got a feeling that everything around here ain't exactly what it seems. Some towns get by with ranching, some have a river that brings in trade. Some have a railroad going through them. Some have a sawmill or other industry. I think we got us a town and a county whose backbone is theft and robbery."

"Can we prove it?"

Longarm thought for a few strides. "I don't know. I may have to bend a few laws to do it. That would be about where you come in."

Austin Davis stopped dead in his tracks. "Like hell."

Longarm put the key in his door, unconcerned. "Now, Austin, you wouldn't want to go to prison for failing to obey the orders of a superior in the Marshals' Service, would you?"

Davis said, "You sonofabitch. I knew you was bad news the moment I laid eyes on you."

Longarm pushed the door open. "You don't like bad news, don't read the newspaper." He motioned with his hand. "Let's get sit down with a bottle and try and figure this out."

Chapter 7

They sat down across from each other at the little table in Longarm's room. He had gotten a bottle from his saddlebags and set it between them along with two glasses. Longarm said, "We are going to have to wind this mess up in a hurry. That is the last bottle of good stuff and no more to be had around here. And I'll be damned if I'll drink rotgut just to help out this rotten town and county. We get them in the next two days or I'm going to leave them to their own devices."

Davis reached out and poured them both a drink. "I hate to hear you talking like that, Marshal. A bounty hunter needs some law to make what he does legal. And you are the only law around here, now that you got the sheriff locked up. You up and run off, I might have a hell of a time collecting on this reward paper I got."

Longarm tossed back half of his drink. "I knew I could count on you, Davis, to take an unselfish approach to the matter."

"Well, what have we got? Have we got a starting place?"

"Yeah, I'd say we got a starting place. I'd say the windmill that is pumping all the water is Dalton Diver. But knowing it and proving it are two different matters."

"How you figure he set it up? How you figure he got it going?"

Longarm shrugged one shoulder. "Of course I can only guess at that, but I got to figure that this Vince Diver played a big hand in it. We already agreed that a bunch of Mason County country boys didn't know anything about robbing and stealing and killing. So they got them some help in here to show them how it worked. I think that Vince Diver was the magnet that drew all the rest of the professionals in. I mean, look at the ones that married Diver's daughters. There was somebody named Lester Gaskamp who was supposed to have been killed in the robbery at Junction City about two years ago. She was married to your girl, Rebeccah. By the way, would she talk about him?"

Davis shook his head. "No. And I want to tell you something right now. There was no Lester Gaskamp or any other Gaskamp killed there. The only man killed in that robbery was a lad identified as Willy Bower, and nobody had ever heard of him. There was a man down along the border named Gaskamp done some robbing and rustling, but he disappeared."

"Well, this Lester Gaskamp was supposed to have been a Mason County boy, but I can't find anyone who ever heard of him. I asked the hotel keeper, Jim Jacks, and he's lived here for the last ten years and he don't know who he is."

Davis said, "There was a Archie Bowen killed in a robbery at Brady. That was about a year ago. I had paper on him and I seen the body. The description matched him. I guarantee you he wasn't no Mason County resident."

Longarm took another drink. "Then there was a Jim Squires who was supposed to have run off from a stage holdup on the road from Austin. He married one of Diver's daughters named Salome, but like all the rest, got the ceremony but not the honeymoon."

Austin Davis suddenly laughed. "Jim Squires? Run off from a robbery? I need to go down to my room and get the poster on him. He's wanted for everything but singing too loud in church. I can't imagine him running out on a job."

Longarm made a face. "I'll take your word for it. Hell, if I had a hard, cold fact I wouldn't know what to do with it." He held up a hand and ticked off fingers. "We got Bowen, Gus Horne or Gus White. We got Gaskamp, we got Squires, and we got Dan Hicks and Vince Diver. All of them known bandits. Then we got this Amos Goustwhite who had money and a check on him from the auction house robbery just as Gus White did. That's enough professional bandits for a town this size, wouldn't you say?"

Davis said, "Yes, considering they must have a crew goes around and collects the bodies, like Goustwhite."

"So we got to figure that some of them ain't bandits, at least not full time. We got to figure that some of them are decent citizens right here in Mason County who only slip out every once in a while to hold up the odd bank or stage. Hell!"

"It's a slick little proposition," Davis said. "I don't see no way to get a knife blade in edgewise and peel the cover off the damn thing. Like you say, knowing what's what and proving it are two different matters. And you ain't even named this Shaker fellow you say folks claim is the boss."

"Wayne Shaker." Longarm shook his head. "Hell, I don't even know if he exists." He looked over at Davis. "But one thing I know exists is this gang of outlaws, be they Mason County goat herders or border bandits who have shifted their operations. Before I got sent down here we had better than fifty complaints and requests for help filter down to our office. Letters, telegrams, reports from deputies in the field. Mostly we were hearing from officials and law officers from the towns and counties surrounding this one. Best we can figure, they have robbed somewhere in the neighborhood of over two hundred thousand dollars. You can run a county pretty good on that kind of money.''

Davis got up, put the palms of his hands in the small of his back, and stretched. He said, ''Well, that's fine and dandy knowing what they done. But who is *they* and how are you going to bring them to bay? You got damn few names, none of which you are sure about, and no faces except a couple of dead ones and my memory of what Vince Diver looks like. And Dan Hicks. How you going to herd them up?''

Longarm shook his head. ''I don't know.''

''You need a soft spot.''

''I got a soft spot, but I can't be the one pokes it with a sharp stick.'' He glanced up at Davis. ''I kept wondering what I hired you on for. Now I know. I reckon it's got to be you puts the squeeze on.'' He stared at Austin Davis.

Davis put his hands on the back of his chair. ''Now wait a minute. You going to have to tell me a little more about what you mean by squeezing. I ain't planning on killing nobody if that is what you mean.''

Longarm gave him a sarcastic look. ''How the hell would you get information out of a corpse, Davis? Use some of that stuff you got between your ears.''

''Listen, don't get insulting with me. I hired on, but I can quit just as fast.''

''You can't quit.''

''Why the hell not?''

''It's against the law. Federal law.''

Davis stared at him for a moment. He finally started laughing. ''Longarm, you are full of it, you know that? I see you are not above a little bullying to get your way. Pray tell who is it you intend I should squeeze.''

''The sheriff. Bodenheimer.''

''Oh, the sheriff. That's different.'' Davis walked

around his chair and sat down. He picked up the bottle of Maryland whiskey and poured a generous amount in his glass. "Don't flinch like that, Longarm. Dirty work requires good whiskey."

Longarm sat down. "It ain't like you could appreciate it. Hell, if I hadn't told you you'd have been just as happy with rotgut. You are just drinking that up to spite me."

Davis drank from his glass and then set it down on the table. He wiped his mouth with the back of his hand. "Aaaaaa!" he said with satisfaction. "That is mighty goooood. I reckon I'll need the rest of the bottle for this dirty work."

"Like hell!" Longarm said. He reached out and pulled the half-empty bottle to his side of the table. "You got a mean streak in you, Davis. You know that?"

Davis laughed. "Here's a man talking about squeezing some poor old fat boy till he pops and he accuses me of having a mean streak. You are a stretch, Longarm. A real stretch. By the way, how come you can't do the squeezing your ownself?"

Longarm grimaced. "Because when you make a threat, the party that is being threatened has got to believe you'll do it or else it ain't no good. And Bodenheimer will know I will only go so far. He won't be scared enough. He's got to be more scared by what you are going to threaten him with than he will be about what he thinks that gang will do to him."

"And how come that lets you out?"

"Because I'm a deputy U.S. marshal."

"Well, hell. I'm supposed to be one too. At least a provisional one."

"Yeah, but Bodenheimer don't know it. Besides, I got a kind of reputation. He'll take that into account."

Davis chortled. "I'll say you got a *kind* of reputation. I'd hate to tell you what *kind* I've heard you got."

"Will you take my point?"

Davis waved a hand. "All right, all right. You want me to squeeze the sheriff. How we going to do it?"

Longarm thought a moment. "I figure to take that money and checks over to the Ownsbys' auction barn. I'll get Bodenheimer out of jail. I'll have him in manacles. I don't want you to be seen with us in town, so you join up about two or three miles up the road. I'll just ride on, leaving him in your hands."

"I take it you want him to tell everything he knows."

"Everything. But especially how Dalton Diver and his daughters tie into the midst of this thing."

"How far you want me to go?"

"Well, don't kill him. Maybe back him up against a tree and see how close you can place a bullet next to his head. Now Austin, this is going to take some playacting. I figure you ought to be pretty good at that."

"Well, if you can playact at being a marshal, I reckon I can handle my end."

Longarm gave him a sour look. "Listen, I'm trusting you with an important job. Quit trying to be cute."

"I'm just trying to find out how to go about this. Can I shoot off a finger or two? I hear that works pretty well. Shoot a couple of fingers off the grub hand of that fat boy and I reckon he'd try and turn inside out. Probably confess to anything."

Longarm shook his head. "I wish you had a little better attitude toward this, Austin. I said *threaten* him, not half-kill him."

Davis turned suddenly hard, cold eyes on Longarm. "I don't know about you, pard, but if someone keeps threatening me with his mouth and ain't doing nothing but tongue-whipping me, I'm going to get the idea pretty soon that I ain't afraid at all. I think you better leave this part to me."

Longarm stared at him, startled by the change in the man. He said slowly, "All right. Do what you have to.

Just save me enough to occupy a federal cell in Leavenworth, Kansas.''

Davis's face relaxed a little. "Maybe I won't have to do nothing to him. But I got to know that I can if I have to. That's the way I bluff a threat. There ain't no bluff to it at all. That's what convinces the other party.''

Longarm shook his head. "You are a curious duck. There for about a second or two you looked about half mean."

Davis didn't smile. "I am. I just don't show that half unless I really have to.''

Longarm lit a cigar and looked at him and suddenly laughed. "Austin Davis, you are a fraud. I cannot believe I let you beat me playing poker. Them antics of yours ought not to fool a stepchild.''

Davis said, "You just keep thinking that way, Marshal. I'm anxious as you are to get this business over with and get you back to the poker table. I lied to you about bounty hunting. The real reason I'm here is that I heard you were in town and had some money for a change.''

Longarm stood up. "Let's go. I don't think I can support much more of this kind of talk from you. The floorboards are starting to creak from the load.''

"When are we going to do this?''

"Right now. I'll get the money and checks from the desk clerk and try and learn you your part while I'm at it. Then I'm going to get the sheriff and meet you about two miles out on the Llano road. Try and keep your nerve. This Bodenheimer will be manacled, but he might still be more than you can handle.''

Davis gave him a dry look. "Talk about a load. I can't wait to get shut of this job. The wages I'm drawing, I could starve to death just listening to you talk.''

Longarm thought that Bodenheimer sat a horse like a sack of flour. Or a sack of lard, if there was any such

115

of a thing. They rode out of town on the Llano road, heading for the auction barn. Of course Bodenheimer didn't know he wasn't going to go all the way.

Longarm had taken him out of the jailhouse with his hands manacled in front of him. Bodenheimer, after an early protest and a repeated demand to be set free, had retreated into a sullen silence. Before heading out of town Longarm had ridden him on a circuit of the courthouse square. As the townspeople had stopped to gawk and to stare, Longarm had said, "Look at that, Otis. They see you cuffed. They knew you were in jail, some of them, but now they see you in chains. What do you reckon they are thinking, Otis? Well, I'll tell you. They are thinking that the barn dance is over. They are thinking that the chickens have come home to roost. You are the ringleader of that thieving gang that has been using this county for a hideout and now that is all over. Those people are seeing the ringleader in chains. That means all that fresh money coming in has done dried up. They won't support you, Bodenheimer. Ain't a one of them will back you."

But Bodenheimer hadn't responded. He didn't speak until they were on the road out of town, and that was only to ask where they were going. Longarm had said, "I ought to be taking you to a hanging party, but I'm only taking you over to the sheriff in Llano. Of course *he* might hang you. But I got no say about that."

Bodenheimer had said, "He ain't got no jurisdiction over me."

Longarm had replied, "Well, you can certainly take that up with him when he takes you over. Might be he's a reasonable man and will only break a couple of your arms."

Now they rode along in silence, Bodenheimer sullen and stolid, Longarm wondering if Austin Davis was going to show up at the right time and have his part down and not mess things up by making a fool of himself.

Longarm had called Davis's attitude frivolous; Austin Davis had replied that Longarm didn't know lighthearted and carefree when he saw it.

Longarm was hoping that Bodenheimer was brooding about his trip around the town square. He had done it deliberately, not to ridicule Bodenheimer, though he was willing for that to happen, but to soften him up for what was to come from Austin Davis. Bodenheimer had to believe that the bandit ring was finished and that he was finished and had nothing to lose by spilling what he knew. He'd been kept in the jail for the past forty-eight hours, so he could have no idea what had been the extent of Longarm's investigation. And now Longarm was taking him to the sheriff of another county. Or at least that was what he was supposed to believe.

They'd been riding for about three quarters of an hour, and Longarm was beginning to wonder where Austin Davis was. By his calculation they'd come closer to five miles than two. He wondered if Davis had run into a bottle of whiskey or a poker game he just couldn't pass by. Maybe the damn fool thought Longarm was playing at some sort of game and that he just gave orders for the pleasure of it. He was starting to get a little hot under the collar when he saw his provisional deputy suddenly burst out of a mesquite thicket and come riding straight for them. Longarm stopped his horse, stopping Bodenheimer at the same time. Bodenheimer just stared at Davis as he came riding toward them. Davis jumped his horse up on the road and then reined him in and came to a skidding, rock-scattering stop. He had his revolver drawn. He said, "Hold up there, Marshal."

Longarm said, "Who are you and what do you want?"

"Never mind who I am. What I want is this man." He gestured with his revolver toward Bodenheimer. "I hate to do it, Marshal, but I am going to have to take your prisoner."

Longarm said, "You can't do that. He is a federal prisoner. I can't surrender him." He was noting with approval that Davis was staring at Bodenheimer with that cold, black-eyed look he'd shown Longarm in the hotel room.

Davis said, "I will have this man, Marshal. He is responsible for the death of my wife in a neighboring town when this man's gang pulled a daring daylight robbery."

Longarm thought that "daring daylight robbery" was laying it on a little thick, but then Bodenheimer was a little thick, so it probably didn't matter. Longarm said, "I won't surrender the prisoner."

Davis said, "You have to. I have the drop on you." Longarm glanced at the barrel of Davis's gun. The front sight, called the drop, had been filed off flush with the top of the barrel. It was a practice followed by most men who did business with handguns because a revolver was never aimed so much as instinctively pointed and the front sight was useless and might get hung up as you drew. Longarm had always disagreed with calling the front sight a "drop" after its resemblence to half a raindrop or teardrop. Longarm always thought it looked more like a half of a penny. But then, he supposed, you couldn't go around saying, "Hands up! I've got the half-penny on you!"

Now he said, "All right, stranger. I have no choice. You do have the drop on me. There is nothing I can do."

Davis said, "Ride on ahead, Marshal. Your work with this man is over. I'm taking on his future."

"You mean just ride off and leave him here with you?"

"That is what I mean, Marshal. You have no choice."

Longarm had been watching Bodenheimer. The sheriff had been glancing back and forth between them as they had enacted their little drama. Other than looking mildly surprised when Austin Davis had first ridden up, he had not shown any emotion. But now, as Longarm started his horse off, he suddenly cried out, "Marshal, what are you about here?"

Longarm turned and looked back at him. "I'm about to ride off and leave you in the hands of this man whose wife was killed as an innocent bystander in one of those robberies you arranged."

Bodenheimer glanced at Davis and then back to Longarm. He said, "You can't! I'm yore prisoner! This man is liable to do me serious harm. You can't leave me!"

Longarm said, "You should have thought of that, Otis, before you started all this mess. If I were you I'd just pray he gives you a quick end. He looks pretty damn vicious to me. Lord knows he is ugly enough."

He put spurs to his horse before Bodenheimer could reply or before Austin Davis could rise to his last remark. He rode at a gallop for a quarter of a mile before he slowed his horse and looked back. He could see Austin Davis taking Bodenheimer off the road and into the thickets and hills of the rough country.

They had decided between themselves that it should take Longarm about two hours to make it to the auction barn and then back to meet Austin Davis and Bodenheimer. Of course that didn't allow for any time talking to Ownsby, who Longarm knew would want to discuss the latest developments in his robbery. But since there hadn't been any developments Longarm was willing to talk about, he didn't reckon to spend much time at the auction barn. Consequently, he had urged Austin Davis to get right to work on Bodenheimer. "It will take you half an hour to get through the fat so you can find a nerve to twinge."

But Davis had claimed he was going to spend the first hour just staring at the sheriff. "You've seen that look of mine. Makes women melt and strong men seek shelter. You may not believe this, but I one time killed an entire field of knee-high cotton with this very look. And done it in less than five minutes by my watch.''

Longarm was looking forward to finishing the job, and not just so he could go home to Colorado. He was seriously interested in getting shut of Mister Davis and his "lighthearted and carefree" ways. He was also, if matters worked out the way he planned, looking forward to giving Mister Austin Davis quite a shock at the conclusion of the affair. He didn't know how Mister Davis felt about surprises, but he was looking forward to having the opportunity to see if he took it in his lighthearted and carefree fashion. He doubted that he would.

It was close on to the two hours as he approached the stretch of road where Austin Davis had intercepted them and taken Bodenheimer off his hands. He was very hopeful that Davis had managed to turn the sheriff around and get something useful out of him, something he could use.

He slowed his horse to a walk and began looking for Davis. If he didn't see him soon, he planned to stop and wait on the road. The country was thick with brush and slashed with cuts and draws. He had no intention of going off the road to try to locate the pair in such country.

His wait was a short one. Within five minutes Austin Davis and his prisoner emerged from the tangle of bushes and weeds that lined the road. Longarm was startled to see that Bodenheimer looked almost exactly the same. He didn't appear to have even picked up any extra dust as a result of his ordeal. And from what Longarm could see, he was certainly not missing any fingers or any other body parts. As they rode up Austin Davis said, "Had to make sure it was you. Can't be too careful in these parts. Lot of road agents about, the sheriff was just telling me.''

Longarm gave him a fierce glare. "Well?''

Austin Davis rode his horse up close to Longarm's so that he and the marshal were facing each other. Davis said, "He's willing to tell us what he knows, but he needs a guarantee. I told him I thought we could work something out."

Davis had left Bodenheimer sitting his horse some ten yards away. The horse's head was drooping and so was Bodenheimer's. Longarm said, "Hell, I didn't send you into that brush to bargain with the sonofabitch! What the hell did you and him do, have a game of cards?"

Davis said patiently, "I seen right off that he was a good deal scareder of the folks he was in with than he was of us. Wasn't ten minutes before he seen through our little ruse. He knows we won't kill him, but he also knows that the other side *will* kill him. So I set in to see if we couldn't arrive at a mutually satisfiable arrangement."

"You did what!"

"I set out to horse-trade with him."

"I see." Longarm was still glaring at Davis, who was pretending not to notice. "I take it you never pulled a gun on him, never dirtied your fists, never threatened to skin him alive, never even showed him a knife, and didn't build a fire and take his boots off and hold his feet close?"

Davis looked away. "Didn't see no need."

"Then what in hell did I hire you for? Hell, I could have gone back there and tried to reach a *mutually satisfiable* arrangement with the bastard. Davis, I've half a mind to lock you in jail and half a mind to drag you behind my horse for a mile or two. What the hell kind of guarantee does he want?"

Davis pulled a face. "He wants safety. He wants you to get him out of here."

"Is that all?"

"Just about."

Longarm glanced over at Bodenheimer, who was sitting placidly on the back of his horse. "Did you tell him our little plot?"

Davis shook his head. "Didn't have to. You're right. You have got a reputation, only this time it didn't serve you so well. Old Bodenheimer ain't as dumb as you think. He said you would have never have let me approach with a drawn gun. That you'd have done something before I ever got close."

Longarm gave his provisional deputy a sour look. "How does *that* make you feel? A man like the sheriff seeing something you ought to have known. What came over you to come riding up here with a drawn gun? Hell!"

Davis took a small cigarillo out of his pocket and lit it with a big match. He said, "Wouldn't have made a damn bit of difference. Bodenheimer told me straight off he knew I was in with you. He said you would have never surrendered a prisoner so easily. Now who's so damn smart? Seeing this whole matter was your idea. He told me point-blank he didn't think I'd do much to him, but it didn't matter because he wasn't going to open his mouth so long as he was in Mason County. Said he'd rather I killed him outright than left him for the dogs that would have got after him. Custis, this is the situation. Can't be changed."

"And he wants out of here?"

"What he says."

"Bring him over."

When he was facing Bodenheimer Longarm said, "What have you got to tell me?"

Bodenheimer shifted his eyes back and forth from Davis to Longarm. He said, "I ain't got nothin' to tell you without you give me your word to see me safe out of here."

"All right. I'll send you to Kansas. You ever been to Kansas?"

Bodenheimer said stolidly, "That there is where the

federal pen is. Leavenworth. I ain't wantin' to go to no prison."

"Then what do you want?"

Bodenheimer's eyes shifted again. "I want you to get me out of here and turn me loose. Out of this county. My life ain't worth a plugged nickel as it is. Soon as you throwed me in jail I was expectin' to be killed at any hour. Then you rode me around the square. That done it."

Longarm thought a moment. "Have you got enough to trade for that? Me turning you loose?"

Bodenheimer licked his lips. "You want who be behind this, don't you? Behind the thieving an' whatnot."

"Yes."

"I can tell you that. And I can tell you how it started and how they do it."

"That's pretty good trading material. Start telling."

"I want your word you'll see me safe out. Safe out of Mason."

Longarm shrugged. "You got it. I give you my word I'll see you safe out of Mason."

"And no federal prison."

Longarm smiled slightly. "No federal prison. Unless you ask for it."

"What's that? Unless I ask for it?"

Longarm nodded. "Yeah, you never know. It might be just the place you'll want to go."

Bodenheimer still looked puzzled, but Austin Davis patted him on the back, winking at Longarm as he did, and said, "Now Otis, me and you done got to be pretty good friends in a pretty short time, ain't we?"

Bodenheimer nodded dumbly. "I guess," he said hesitantly. "You said I could trust Marshal Long. You said it was the only way out for me."

"Well, can't you see that? You don't want to get hurt. You don't want to have that bunch tear you in two between a team of horses, do you? Now you already told me a good bit of it. Whyn't you go ahead and unburden yourself to the good marshal here. He'll see you right."

Longarm stared at Davis. He thought that next he'd be offering Bodenheimer a shoulder to cry on. Longarm said, "If you got anything worth telling, now is the time to do it. I want to know who is behind all this robbery. It's organized. Don't take no U.S. senator to know that."

Bodenheimer glanced over at Austin Davis. Davis nodded. Bodenheimer said hesitantly, "Well, I guess you'd have to say that the mayor and the president of the bank and Dalton Diver was at the bottom of it."

Longarm stared at him. "The mayor? The president of the bank?"

"Yeah, it was them two come to me and said what they had in mind. Said it was Dalton Diver's idea to help the county with some fresh money. But they said it wouldn't work if the gang couldn't count on a safe place to light between robberies. They said it was going to be a pretty rough bunch and I'd be a lot better going along with it rather than getting killed. They said that would happen for shore, and they'd just put somebody in my job who would carry along, so what was the use of my battling agin it."

Longarm said dryly, "Naturally you saw the sense in going along with that."

Bodenheimer said, a whine in his voice, "I couldn't fight all of 'em, could I?"

Longarm gave a disgusted snort, but Austin Davis patted Bodenheimer on the back and said, "Marshal, let him get it out. Be good for him. This man has had a hard row to hoe. Go light on him."

Longarm looked up at the sky and shook his head, but didn't speak other than to tell Bodenheimer to get on with it.

Davis said, "Now when was this, Otis?"

Bodenheimer shrugged. "Little over two year ago. The mayor said the way it was going to work was they'd bring in some pretty tough boys to do the actual work, but they'd get some Mason County boys as part of it so the home folks would feel like they was a part of the doings and wouldn't kick up no sand.''

Longarm said, ''Who was going to bring in the professionals?''

''That would have been Mister Diver's doin' on account he knowed some.''

''Who is Vince Diver?''

The sheriff hesitated for a second, and then looked down at the ground and shook his head. ''I don't know. Never heered the name.''

''Then what were the names of some of the toughs they brought in?''

Again the sheriff shook his head and studied the ground. ''I don't know. They thought it best if I wasn't on to the name of nobody.''

Longarm made a disgusted sound. ''Oh, bullshit! How was you supposed to know who to leave alone if you didn't know who they were?''

Bodenheimer looked up. ''They just said to leave everybody alone. Just go on like I had been.''

''Which hadn't been much to begin with.'' Longarm stared at the man a moment more. Finally he said, ''What about the Mason County boys? Who are they?''

The sheriff shrugged. ''Nobody much. Just ne'er-do-wells that mostly hung around town and played cards and drank whiskey. The Goustwhite brothers, Amos and Emil. Then there was Ernie Abshier and Lester Gaskamp, though it be hard to say if Lester was a Mason boy or not. His folks had moved away a long time ago. Then there was Bolton Surges and Tom Wilton. Wilton got kilt. And I think Surges didn't care for the business. But none of them amounted to a hill of beans. They was all in the back and never took no hand in the planning of matters.''

''What about Wayne Shaker? He is supposed to be a

Mason boy as well as the leader of the bunch."

The sheriff shook his head. "I've heered the name, but I've never clapped eyes on the man."

"What's the banker's name?"

"That would be Mister Crouch, Mister Ernest Crouch. He's the president of the bank, the Mason State Bank."

"What in the hell is a banker doing mixed up in this?"

Bodenheimer looked up surprised. "Why, how else would we spread the money around so it would do ever'body some good? Folks go to the bank an' Mister Crouch, he loans 'em money against hard times, like we been havin' lately. Or he loans some to the city and the mayor sees it gets spread around. You see how it works? Makes it good for ever'body. That's plain as paint."

Longarm said, "How about the folks in the other towns where the robberies took place? Does it make it good for them?"

Bodenheimer frowned. "Well, that would be their lookout, wouldn't it."

"Yeah. And mine. What did you get out of this, Otis? I'm about to figure out who the big winners were, but what about you?"

Bodenheimer shrugged. "They let me keep my job. An' the mayor let me put two of my kinfolk to work."

"That all?"

Bodenheimer looked uneasy. "Well, they did gimme a twenty-five-dollar-a-month rise in my salary. An' they started furnishin' me an' my two deputies with horses."

Austin Davis laughed. "I bet that wasn't no hardship—the horses, I mean. Probably had more stolen stock than they knew what to do with."

Longarm said to Bodenheimer, "One thing I ain't exactly clear on. The money went to the bank, to Mister Ernest Crouch. But I don't believe that he talked a bunch of hard men into giving him the proceeds from their robberies. Most robbers are stupid, but I can't believe anybody is that stupid.''

Bodenheimer looked startled. ''Oh, no, Marshal. Them robbers taken their cut. Land-a-mercy, naturally they did. What the mayor and the banker done was to charge them for hidin' out in Mason County. Sort of a fee or a rent. Don't you see?''

''How much was it?''

Bodenheimer shook his head. ''Now that I don't be knowing.''

Austin Davis said, ''Otis, one thing as has puzzled me is where the Diver girls come into this business. They kept marrying into the gang, but the marriages never come to nothing. What was that all about?''

Bodenheimer shook his head again. ''I couldn't tell you that, Marshal Smith. That was ol' Dalton Diver's work. Didn't have nothin' to do with our arrangement. I'd reckon that was just his way of making a little something on the side. We all thought it was pretty fine because it took more of the money out of the actual robbers' hands and kept it here.''

''What do you know about a Mister Summers drowning?'' Longarm asked. ''About two or three months ago. That was handy as hell for Dalton Diver and his daughter Hannah.''

The sheriff was defensive. ''Now I don't know nothin' 'bout that and I don't want to know. I tol' my deputies to steer clear of the business and that is a fact. What they wanted to do amongst themselves was no affair of our'n.''

Longarm thought for a moment, and then he glanced at Austin Davis. Davis just made a shrugging motion as if that was all as far as he was concerned. Longarm said, ''All right, Bodenheimer, get off your horse.''

Chapter 8

The sheriff stood there uncertainly, looking as if he were waiting for further instructions. None came. Austin Davis rode over, gathered up the reins of Bodenheimer's horse, and turned back toward town. Longarm wheeled his mount and started off in company with Austin Davis. The sheriff watched them dumbly for a few seconds, and then he said loudly, "Wait a minute! Wait a minute! What are you doing?"

Longarm was about ten yards away. He turned in his saddle and looked back at the fat man wearing manacles. He said, "Why, what you asked, Otis. I'm seeing you safe out of Mason. You're out of Mason and you're safe. What else you want?"

Bodenheimer had a stricken look on his face. "But you can't leave me afoot out here like this! Somebody will come along and kill me. I can't walk in these boots, and you still got me chained!"

Austin Davis said, "There is just no pleasing some people. Hell, Marshal, it doesn't appear that Otis is grateful to you for his freedom."

Bodenheimer said, "You can't leave me afoot!"

Longarm said, "Bodenheimer, you the same as told me the horse you are riding is stolen. As a law officer I can't let you ride off on a stolen horse.''

"But you promised you'd see me safe. Didn't he, Marshal Smith?''

Longarm turned and looked at Austin Davis. "Did I promise that, *Marshal Smith*?''

Austin Davis did not even have the good grace to look ashamed. He said, "Well, maybe in a way you did. But he looks pretty safe right now. And he is free and he is out of Mason.''

Bodenheimer's voice rose in a kind of wail. "I meant see me safe someplace else than Mason *County*. Hell, I ain't even out of the county! I meant see me safe someplace I can stay! I can't stay on this road.''

Longarm turned his horse around so he was facing the sheriff. "Listen, Bodenheimer, what am I supposed to do with you? I ain't got time to carry you to a place where you can be safe. I don't know what safe is for you. I told you earlier that you might want to go to prison, might ask to go to Kansas. Is that what you want? Because that is about the only safety I can offer you.''

Behind him Austin Davis said, "Marshal, I've had a thought.''

Longarm looked back. "And what would that be, Marshal Smith?''

"Well, why don't you let him go back to sheriffing?''

Longarm was startled. This had been no part of their plans. He said, "Marshal, why in hell would I want to arrest a law officer for being a crook and then give him his job back?''

Davis said, "Well, perhaps he's learned his lesson. And perhaps he could be of some help to us. Maybe he'd like to redeem himself and be an honest sheriff.''

Longarm looked at Bodenheimer and then back at Davis with amazement clear on his face. He said, "One of us is talking like they've been eating loco weed, and I don't think it is me. Why in hell would you want me to let him come back as sheriff? He ought to be a sheriff, all right, in a cell in Leavenworth. Malfeasance in office is a federal crime that will get you ten years breaking rocks.''

Davis said, ''Yeah, I know you got him dead to rights, Marshal Long, but hell, everybody makes a mistake now and then. It ain't like he was one of the ones with a gun in his hand, shooting up towns. And it ain't like he made a big profit. Twenty-five-dollar-a-month raise? That ain't exactly high cotton.''

Longarm looked at Bodenheimer. The sheriff was standing there, anxiety on his face, wringing his hands together in spite of the manacles. Longarm said, ''Hell, he'd give us away in a minute. Look, I'm trying to put people in jail, not let them out. Hell!''

Davis said, ''Look at it this way, Custis. You may have already spooked that mayor and the banker. But you let ol' Otis here come on back in his job—and in your company, why, that ought to sooth some ruffled feathers right there. Remember, we still got quite a few quail to flush yet.''

''Yeah,'' Longarm said thoughtfully. ''But I don't know if I want old Otis here flushing them for me. He is likely to flush them way before I'm ready.''

''I got a feeling old Otis here will do just about what he's told. That and nothing more. Ain't that right, Otis?''

Bodenheimer's mouth was hanging open and his eyes were wide with hope. He took a step forward. ''Oh, yessir! Yessir! Marshal, I'd give anything fer another chance. I know I done wrong, but I didn't see no way out. You could give me one.''

Longarm sat, thinking. On the one hand he hated to see Bodenheimer get off with nothing more than a few days in jail. But he still did have quite a few chickens yet to get in the henhouse, and the sight of Bodenheimer returned to good standing might ease some of the fidgets he imagined were running through certain quarters. And in the end, his real interest was in stopping dead the gunhands who had actually done the robbing and killing. Of course he meant to get Dalton Diver and the banker and the mayor in the same net. Maybe Davis was right, much as he hated to admit it. Longarm said, "What if I set him back up and he betrays us?"

"Then gutshoot him. Give him a couple of days to die slow and painfully. That will teach him not to suck eggs."

Longarm looked back at Austin Davis. "Thank you, Marshal Smith. By the way, since we are new on this assignment together, I never did get your first name."

Davis gave him an innocent look. "It's John."

"Honest John, no doubt."

Davis looked modest. "They mostly call me that."

Longarm said, "Well, Honest John, I hope for your sake that you are right about this matter, because it is going to be your nut in the wringer if something goes wrong and it leads back to old Otis here."

Bodenheimer said, "I swear it, Marshal. I swear you can set store by me. I won't let you down." He was so agonized that drops of sweat were standing out on his big forehead even with a cool breeze blowing.

Longarm looked at him sourly. "One thing I ain't heard about as much as I want to, and that is your deputies. How deep are they in this?"

Bodenheimer took another step forward. "Marshal, I can nearly swear that the two what is blood kin to me ain't in none of it. They ain't smart enough. And I made sure they never come close to being exposed to it at all."

"They ain't smart enough?" Longarm leaned out of the saddle toward the sheriff and put his hand to his ear. "Come again? You are talking about how smart someone is? Otis, that has got to make me ask you how you would know.''

The sheriff looked down. "I know how it looks. But it's hard makin' a living around here, and I just put them boys to work kind of for no reason. They ain't really deputies. They don't know nothing about the law.''

"But they carry guns.''

"Yeah, but they ain't mean or nothin' like that. It's just a job for them. It was part of the deal for me keeping my eyes and ears closed. Of course I can't say about Melvin Purliss. I don't know all that much about him. He was kind of part of the deal. Now he is a capable hand. He's been in law work before.''

Longarm glanced at Austin Davis. "Little Melvin Purliss? He's been a lawman? Hell, I thought he was another one of your charity cases.''

The sheriff shook his head. "Nosir. The mayor and the council thought I ought to have one deputy capable of keeping the peace and they give me Melvin, oh, a year, year and a half back.''

Longarm nodded at Austin Davis. "Well, at least we got a little help. But I never thought it would be Purliss.''

Davis said, "Well, what are you going to do? It's getting on toward noon. We need to get moving.''

Longarm dug in his pocket and found the key to the manacles. He pitched it in the dust in front of Bodenheimer. But before the sheriff could lean over to pick it up Longarm said, "Get one thing straight, Otis. And remember it. If you forget everything else in your life, you had best remember this.''

Bodenheimer straightened up. "Yessir.''

Longarm's words were even and low. "You break my trust, you betray me in any way, you upset the applecart in the slightest, and I will make you sorry you were ever born. Do you understand that?''

"Yessir.'' Bodenheimer was trembling.

"Do you believe it?"

"Oh, yes, sir. Yessir, I shore do."

Longarm turned to Austin Davis. "Give him his horse, Marshal Smith. And then let us me and you ride on back into town. Bodenheimer, you follow at about a mile."

As they rode the several miles back to town Austin Davis said, "Cap'n, they is a few things you ain't exactly explained to my satisfaction. For one thing, we have got an awful lot of beaver to trap at the same time. There's the mayor and the banker and especially Dalton Diver. But that ain't mentioning the ones we really want, the gunhands that have done the actual work. We don't know what most of them look like. We know damn few names, and we don't even know if them are the right names. And we sure as hell don't know where to find these folks. Never mind how we are going to take them, first we got to find them. How is all of that supposed to happen?"

Longarm glanced over at Davis. "Well, Marshal Honest John Smith, the knowing and the doing of this proposition is why I'm the boss and you are a provisional deputy. You just keep doing what you are doing and leave the thinking to me. I'm afeared you might hurt yourself if you went to studying on matters. And you better damn well pray that you are right about Bodenheimer."

"Well, what else were you going to do with him? You damn sure didn't have time to take him to Austin where the nearest federal court is. Leave him out there on that road afoot? Hell, somebody might have come along, and then he damn sure would have gotten back into town and warned everybody he named."

"All right, all right," Longarm said. "Let's say that for once you were right. I don't understand how it happened, but I guess it did." Then he glanced over at Davis, taking in his flat-crowned, stiff, wide-brimmed black hat. He said, "What are you doing up here wearing a border hat? I been meaning to ask you that the first time I laid eyes on you in that poker game at the saloon. You figure it makes you look tough? Makes you look like you don't know how to buy a hat, is what it does."

Davis looked unconcerned. "At least I ain't called Longarm because my first name is Custis. Lord, what a burden that must have been to you as a child."

Longarm said, "I wouldn't be talking about names, *Marshal* Smith. Do you know what the penalty is for impersonating a federal officer?"

"No, but I bet you do. Lord knows you've been getting away with it long enough."

"Me and you," Longarm said grimly, "are going to play some head-up poker when this is over. Maybe for your life."

"You just can't admit I done a good job with Bodenheimer, can you. It'd kill you, wouldn't it. You'd fall off that horse and drop down dead in the road if you had to admit to such a thing, wouldn't you."

Longarm just gave him a look.

When they were a quarter of a mile out of town, Longarm pulled them up. They stood in the middle of the road waiting for Bodenheimer to catch up. Longarm said to Davis, "Soon as we get squared away I am going out to Hannah's house and bring her into jail. You are going out to fetch that Rebeccah in."

Davis's eyes got wide. "Are you crazy? Hell, send me after Billy the Kid. I'd much rather take him on. Custis, that woman is a wildcat."

"I don't care what she is. You bring her into town. She is going to jail. And I'm going to send the sheriff and his deputies to fetch in Salome and the other one, Sarah. Then tonight, me and you is going to see Dalton Diver. I got to get this thing brought to a head. And in a hurry. I'm tired of fooling with it."

Davis looked back down the road where Bodenheimer was coming at a trot, bouncing up and down in the saddle. He said, "You ain't no more ready than I am. I swear I don't believe I ever fetched up in such a town like this afore in my life. Look at the sheriff. That poor pony of his is going to be swaybacked before the week is out."

Longarm didn't speak again until the sheriff had joined them. Bodenheimer, even though it was too cool for sweat, pulled a big bandanna out of his pocket and swabbed his face. They all could see the tops of the town buildings just around a curve. Longarm said, "Now Otis, I want you to get it straight in your mind that you and I have come to an agreement that you are innocent of any wrongdoing and I have turned you loose. That is what you are to tell anyone who asks you. But don't volunteer nothing, understand?"

The sheriff nodded.

"And you avoid the mayor and the bank president as if they were carrying the plague. I got a feeling you ain't a very good liar, Otis, so you keep temptation out of your way. You understand?"

"Yessir." The sheriff nodded again.

Longarm looked at him for a long moment. Finally he said, "I ain't never done nothing like this before, Bodenheimer. You understand?"

"Yessir."

"Now I have warned you about giving us away in any way. Any loose talk, any thought of betrayal will spell your end. You understand?"

"Yessir."

Longarm was still staring at him. "You life is literally in your mouth. Keep that in mind."

"Yessir."

Davis said, "Sounds like he's got his part down. Yessir. Yessir."

Longarm ignored him. He said to Bodenheimer, "Now, we are going to start this thing off as soon as we get into town. I am going to go out and bring Miss Hannah in. Marshal Smith is going to fetch in Miss Rebeccah." He jabbed Bodenheimer in the chest. "You and your three deputies are going to go out and fetch in Miss Sarah and Miss Salome. You are to bring them in and put them in jail."

Bodenheimer's eyes got as round as his face. He said, stuttering, "Wha-wha-what? Bring in Dalton Diver's daughters and put them in jail?"

"Yes." Longarm looked at him hard. "And this is something you ain't going to do halfway or mess up, Bodenheimer. You don't bring those two women back to town, it will be better for you that you don't come back at all."

"But-but . . ." Bodenheimer blinked his eyes like he was about to get tearful. "But how am I supposed to do that? Dalton Diver will have my hide nailed to his barn door! I'm scairt of that man, and so is everybody else."

"You better be more scared of me, Otis. Now. What you do is, you go to Miss Sarah's house and tell her that Miss Hannah is at the jail with their father, Dalton, and you and your deputies have been sent to fetch her and Miss Salome. If they ask, and they will, what it is all about, you just tell them that you don't know. Tell them you are doing what their daddy told you to do. Say you think it has something to do with their half-brother. But don't explain any more than that." He gave the sheriff a sardonic look. "Remember, they will still think you are a crooked lawman running an errand for their daddy."

Bodenheimer nodded slowly as he took it in. "Just tell them their daddy wants them in town."

"At the jail."

"At the jail." He nodded slowly once more. He

looked at Longarm. "What do I do then? They'll see that their daddy ain't there."

"You put them in a jail cell. You tell them they are under federal arrest. You tell them I have ordered their arrest."

Bodenheimer leaned backward so far he almost fell out of his saddle. He said, "Put them in a jail cell! Dalton Diver's daughters!"

"Yes."

Bodenheimer was visibly trembling. He said, "I ain't sure I can do that. How we supposed to get them in there?"

Longarm said, irritation in his voice, "Bodenheimer, if four strong men can't put two women in a cell, then you'd better get in it yourself and throw away the key. You got this one chance. Screw it up and you'll be doing twenty-five years in Leavenworth Prison. Do you understand me?"

The sheriff's face worked for a moment, but then he finally nodded. "Yessir. Tell 'em they daddy wants them at the jail and then put them in a cell. Yessir. I don't know how my deputies is going to feel about this."

"They better feel the way you tell them. Now let's get into town."

As they rode toward the jail Austin Davis said, "Well, I'm glad to hear I'm supposed to get Miss Rebeccah in here by sleight of hand. I thought you meant for me to manhandle her."

Longarm gave him a look. "Why, Marshal Smith, I'd never give you a job I knew you couldn't handle. And in your case the word is boyhandle."

Austin Davis nodded placidly. "Go on with them kind of remarks. I think it is pretty clear who has done the most to get information about the way this gang works. Had been you, you'd still be back there torturing and threatening Otis."

They pulled up in front of the jail. Bodenheimer dismounted and looked questioningly at Longarm. The marshal said, "Go on in and let your deputies loose. Send Melvin Purliss out right now. Next time I see you, you'd better have them two women in jail cells."

Bodenheimer ducked his head and said, "Yessir." After that he stepped up on the boardwalk and disappeared into the jailhouse.

Davis said, "If Bodenheimer wasn't so pitful he'd be funny. You want me to take on off and get Rebeccah?"

Longarm nodded. "You might as well. And once you get back, stay here at the jail until I get in. After that we'll wait for Bodenheimer and his party, and then me and you are going to go see Dalton Diver."

Austin Davis was wheeling his horse away from the hitching post. He said, "That ought to be right interesting." He left, riding northeast out of town.

Melvin Purliss came out the door and walked hesitantly over to Longarm. "Sheriff said you wanted to see me, Marshal. Is Otis sheriff again?"

Longarm nodded. "Yes. For the time being. Listen, Purliss, you and him and the other two deputies are going out to get two of Dalton Diver's daughters and bring them back to town."

Purliss looked slightly startled. "We are?"

"Yes. At my orders. Now, there can be no slipups on this matter. I want you to keep a close eye on the sheriff. He knows what to do and I want you to see that he does it. If anything goes wrong, I will hang the four of you from the tallest tree I can find. And if there ain't a tree tall enough, I'll drag you behind an ox. You understand me?"

Purliss looked uncertain still. But he said, "I reckon so, Marshal. How we supposed to do this?"

"Dalton Diver is coming in and he wants to see his

daughters in a bunch. I'm going for one myself and so is the other marshal. Listen, how many men does Dalton Diver have working for him at his place?''

Purliss shrugged. "Not many. A couple or three. They are just general hands.''

"How come you never told me you had law experience before you came here?''

It took Purliss by surprise. He said, "Why, why, why, I never knowed it mattered.''

"Where were you? What town?''

Purliss blinked. "Uh, here and there.''

"Here and there where?''

Purliss looked everywhere but at Longarm. He finally said, "Well, Denton. That's up in North Texas.''

"I know where Denton is. Who was the sheriff there?''

"Uhhhhh . . .'' Purliss blinked. "Uh, George Wright.''

Longarm looked at him, frowning slightly. There was something wrong with the answer, but he didn't quite know what it was. Neither did he have time to study on the matter. He said, "You see to the sheriff and those other deputies. You understand me?''

"Yessir. Yessir, Marshal.''

Longarm nodded, and turned his horse out into the street. He calculated it was pushing for two o'clock in the afternoon. Neither he nor Davis had had any lunch, but that would have to wait. He had Hannah Diver to worry about first.

She had the door open and was standing in the doorway almost before he could dismount in front of her cabin. Behind him he could hear the rush and roar of the river as it banged and tore against the rocks and the sandbars and banks. He reckoned there were probably trout in the stream. It looked like one of the little rivers he was used to seeing in Colorado.

He walked up to her. She was wearing the same wrapper she'd had on before. It had been hastily and carelessly donned. Some of her was in it, but not all. He could feel a swelling in his groin, but he had no time for that. He was here to take her to jail and he had to keep reminding himself of that.

She said, "Laws, I've had me an itch I can't scratch ever since you left! Where you been?"

He said, "Now, Hannah, we can't do—"

But he got no further. She grabbed him by the front of the vest, pulled him through the door, and then threw her arms around his neck and fastened her mouth to his. He resisted her probing tongue for as long as he could stand it, but rising desire finally made him join with her, his own mouth covering hers and forcing it open wider and wider. But when he could, he came up for breath and pushed her back gently. He said, "Hannah, we can't do this. We got some business to tend to."

She said, "Mister, I'm all the business you can handle right now." With a quick move she undid the sash of her wrapper and then shrugged it off her shoulders and stood before him naked. He stared at her, unable now to control the desire that was racing through him like a fever. He stared at her belly, noting how the lightness of her skin muted into the light brown hair of her bush, growing darker as it wove its way toward the thatch that sprouted at the joining of her legs. She came toward him and he said, a little breathlessly, "Hannah, now wait . . ."

But she was tearing at the buckle of his gunbelt. Before he realized what she was doing, he felt the weight leave his hips and heard the clump as his gun kit hit the floor in its holster. He said, "Hannah! That's a good way to explode a gun."

She had fallen to her knees, working at his pants belt buckle. She said, "The only gun I want to explode is in here."

Then, faster than he would have thought possible, she

had opened his belt, unbuttoned his jeans, and jerked them down around his knees. He felt a shiver of sheer pleasure run through his whole body as she took him in her mouth and began making little sucking sounds. He said, "Oh, oh, oh! Hannah! Be careful! Wait a minute, wait a minute!"

With all the strength he could manage, he reached down, took her by the shoulders, and pulled her up. For a second he bent his mouth to her two erect, hard nipples, the caressing bringing little sounds of pleasure from her. Then he turned her around, facing away from him, and bent her over at the waist, spreading her legs with his hand. She had long legs and was easy to reach. He guided himself into her, surprised at how open and wet she already was. She seemed to get ready faster than any woman he'd ever known.

He held her at the abdomen with both his hands and pulled her buttocks back into him. As he penetrated her, going deeper and deeper with each thrust, she cried out in unison with the movements.

She was leaning forward, her hands on her knees, pushing back at him. As their excitement mounted in tandem, she began letting out little cries that gradually began to run together. He tried to hold himself back, and could feel her begin to tremble. Then it seemed as if they both exploded at the same time. He was dimly aware of a loud screaming and of his own breath and pulse pounding in his ears. He could feel her violent maneuvers, and then his legs turned to jelly and he crumpled, pulling her down with him. He landed on his back on the hardwood floor of the cabin, and she landed on top of him. He was still inside her.

He rested for a moment and then, when he could, lifted her gently off him and set her on the floor at his side. Then, awkwardly, he struggled to his feet, pulled up his jeans, and buttoned and buckled himself as fast as he could.

From the floor Hannah said, "I want some more."

He shook his head and bent down to retrieve his gun-belt. As he buckled it on he said, "Honey, we can't. I just come to get you. We've got to go into town."

"Into town?" She frowned. "Whatever for?"

"I don't really know. But your daddy and your other sisters are at the jailhouse. The sheriff just asked if I'd come escort you in."

"Whaaat!" She scrambled to her feet and put her hands on her hips. "What do you mean my daddy and my sisters are at the jailhouse! What in hell is going on?"

He shook his head. "I don't know. It's something about your half-brother. That's all I know."

"Half-brother?" Her eyes got cloudy and suspicious. "I ain't got no half-brother."

He shrugged. "Then don't go. All I know is your daddy wants you there. You want me to tell him you ain't coming?"

She bit her lip. "My daddy is at the jailhouse? *My* daddy?"

"Dalton Diver. Ain't he your daddy?"

"Weeell, yes. But what is he doing at the jailhouse? If he's in any trouble I'll kill that lard-butt sheriff."

Longarm shook his head. "He's not in any trouble. Like I say, I don't know anything about it. I just happened by and they asked if I'd take word to you. I understand your other sisters are either there or are on the way."

"What other sisters? You mean the ones still at home?"

Longarm shook his head. "No. I think it's Rebeccah and Sarah and Salome. You want me to saddle you a horse? Or hitch up a buggy?"

As they were getting ready to leave, Longarm tried to make small talk to keep her mind occupied. He said, "You know, funny thing. You don't sound like

142

you are from Texas. You got an accent like you hear up north.''

She said, ''Naw, I'm from Texas. It must have been from hearin' Daddy all them years. He used to live in Michigan. That's way up north.''

''I know where it is,'' Longarm said. ''What in hell was he doing up there?''

''Aw, him and his church was runnin' from religious per-persah . . . Something.''

''Religious persecution?''

''Yeah, that's it. They couldn't practice their own religion where they was. Folks wouldn't have it. So him and the whole bunch of 'em up and moved to a place in Michigan that nobody else wanted.''

Longarm frowned. ''What was his religion that he was persecuted?''

''They was Shakers.''

''Shakers?'' Longarm thought for a moment. ''I don't reckon I ever heard of them. What set them off, say, from Baptists or Lutherans or whatnot?''

She was busy brushing her hair. She said into the mirror, ''Well, they believed in share and share alike. But what got 'em into trouble was they carried that over about wives and such.''

''You mean they could have more than one wife?''

''They could have a bunch, I think. Anyway, Daddy didn't mind that sharing all around so much, though he felt they was a bunch didn't come up with their fair share. But then they went to poaching on his wives, so he just took him one and come to Texas. That's what he said. He said he just grabbed up a wife and what kids there was and come to Texas.''

''Were you born in Texas?''

''Aw, yeah. This was all some years back. Better'n twenty, I would reckon. My momma wasn't a Shaker. Daddy come acrosst her here in Texas. I think his Shaker wife passed on over while I was a little girl. I don't recollect her."

"I see," Longarm said slowly.

He didn't say any more about it until they were mounted and riding into town. Then he said casually, "Anyone in your family got the given name of Wayne?"

"Wayne?" She looked at him and laughed. "Marshal, we is all girls. Wayne is a boy's name."

"Yeah," he said. "Guess you're right."

When they walked into the jailhouse only Austin Davis was there. He was leaning up against a desk with his arms closed. Longarm looked at him. "Nobody here yet?"

Davis coughed slightly and signaled Longarm with his eyes. "Just Mister Diver. He's back in one of the cells resting."

"He ain't sick, is he?"

Davis shook his head. "No, no. Not sick. That cell on the left as you go through is open. Door is open. He wanted it that way so he could get some air."

Longarm stared for a second before he realized that Davis was telling him that the door to the first cell on the left was open. It was good information to have, Longarm thought. Miss Hannah was liable to turn into a handful when she realized she had been tricked and was about to occupy a jail cell.

She was looking Austin Davis over. "Who be this?"

Longarm said, "That's another federal marshal, Marshal Smith. Honest John Smith."

"Howdy do," Hannah said.

Austin Davis doffed his hat. "How do you do, Miss Hannah."

"I hope my daddy ain't ailing."

"No, he's just resting." Austin Davis looked over her

head at Longarm. "But I'd hurry on back. The other sisters might be getting here any minute. Might get crowded at the door."

Longarm said, "I better take her in to her daddy."

Davis said, "I'll get the door."

With Davis holding the big, heavy door that separated the cells from the office, Longarm took Hannah by the arm and escorted her through the door just as it opened. He saw the empty cell on his left with the door standing open, and was immediately aware of a sharp outcry to his right. Hannah tried to look around him toward the cell on the right, but he unceremoniously shoved her into the open cell and, while she was still startled, closed the barred door and locked it. As quick as he could, he jerked the key free and stepped back through the big door as Austin Davis shut it behind him.

The thick door cut off most of the screams and cries, but they were both aware of the tumult coming from the cells. Longarm ran his sleeve across his forehead. He said, "Wheee, I don't much care for that brand of work."

"About like putting a bobcat in a burlap bag. And nearly as noisy."

Longarm said, "I got a little glance at Rebeccah. She's as pretty as Hannah, though in a darker way. How'd you make out?"

Davis shrugged. "About like you, except I didn't have nobody to open the big door for me and the cell door was locked." He showed Longarm the side of his neck where it was severely scratched. "I had to hold her whilst I unlocked that cell door. She seen my intent and didn't care for it. By then, of course, she knowed her daddy wasn't here. But it was fine up until then."

"You got here ahead of me." Longarm was thinking guiltily of what had delayed him. "Guess you didn't waste no time."

Davis said, "I got lucky. She was just coming in from a ride when I got there. We just turned around and come on in, though she was suspicious as hell about what her daddy was doing at the jail."

"So was her sister."

Austin Davis reached in his pocket and came out with a cigarillo and a match. He lit the black little cigar and got it drawing. "We going to see ol' Dalton Diver?" he asked.

Longarm nodded toward the cells. "I'd feel better if we waited and made sure we had all our chicks in the coop before we left matters to the sheriff and his boys."

Davis said, "Am I right in thinking why you want the daughters penned up before we see the daddy?"

Longarm nodded. "I would reckon you are. Lord, I am hungry. Are you?"

"We ain't ate since breakfast. But maybe Dalton Diver will give us some supper."

Longarm looked grim. "I would doubt it. This could be a little rough, Austin. He's got three hired hands out there."

Davis was busy looking through the drawers of the sheriff's desk. "Aaah, I figured he'd have a little liquid courage in here." He came out holding a bottle of whiskey. He uncorked it and gave it a smell. "Ain't too bad. Of course it ain't that fancy whiskey of yours." He put the bottle to his lips and took a short drink. He coughed a little and held the bottle out to Longarm. "Ain't the smoothest I ever drank. You want me to hold a gun on you?"

Longarm took the bottle. "Naw, I reckon I can get a swig down on my own." He took two quick swallows out of the bottle and then lowered it. He breathed out, "Aaaaah! For heaven's sake, don't strike an open flame. Whole place will go up."

Austin Davis suddenly looked toward the door.

"Sounds like our party has arrived."

"It's going to be a party, all right. I reckon we better get ready to help them. Though I ain't sure if the six of us can manage it."

Davis said, "I just wish I had me some little corks to shove in my ears. It is going to be a powerful racket when we shove two more in there."

Chapter 9

They rode out of town through the gathering twilight. Longarm calculated it would take them three quarters of an hour to a full hour to reach Dalton Diver's place. He said, "I doubt we'll get there before seven."

Austin Davis said, "After supper. Hell, my stomach thinks my throat has been cut. Maybe they'll have some left over."

Longarm glanced sideways at him. "I doubt you can expect Mister Diver to extend us much hospitality when he finds out what we are there for."

"You reckon he'll crumble?"

Longarm made a shrug. "I don't know. That's up to him. With the evidence I got I can send a number of people to jail. It's all up to Diver what their names are gonna be."

"How many girls left at home?"

"What I understand from Hannah, there are four. I think the oldest is around seventeen, maybe eighteen. The youngest is maybe twelve."

"Then there's four married, or kind of married, around here."

"And the other two have married and moved off. I

don't reckon they count. Maybe Rachel, the one living at Rock Springs.''

Davis said, ''That Shaker business is cute as hell, ain't it? Who would have ever thought of such a thing. I never heard of no Shakers, had you?''

The road narrowed and then forked. Longarm bore them to the left. They were in a grove of mesquite and post oak and it made it seem darker. Longarm said, ''Watch out for that limb on your right. No, I had never heard of no Shakers, though I don't doubt that there are such. But if using that name was Dalton's idea of a little joke, he is going to have a hell of a hard time explaining his way out of it.''

''I guess they got kind of arrogant.''

Longarm glanced over at his riding mate. ''Hell, why shouldn't they? They were like the local sawmill or a silver mine. They were a business, bringing money into the town and the county. Never mind it was other people's money. Hell, they were popular around here. Arrogant? Hell, they were proud. Everybody in this county thanks them. By rights I ought to put every citizen over the age of twelve in jail. That would interfere with their daydream and maybe teach them the difference between right and wrong. I don't ever remember getting so down on a place in all my life.''

''So I take it you are agin this scheme?''

Longarm gave him a sour look, but he doubted Davis could see it in the dim light. ''We're a long ways from wrapping up this particular matter. I'll be glad to joke with you later. Right now I'm tired and hungry and just a little pissed off.''

It was close to an hour later when they spotted lights through the sparse trees. Within another quarter of a mile they could see a big, two-story whitewashed house standing atop a broad little hillock. Behind were several barns and sheds and a few corrals. As they neared, Longarm could see that the central part of the house had once been a simple two-story frame, and that with years and children, wings and such had been added on. It was a common enough practice in the South and the Southwest. They rode directly up to the front steps that led to the big porch running across the front of the house. From the back Longarm could hear a pack of dogs suddenly break into voice. He figured they were coon or fox dogs, and therefore penned up and not likely to come flying around the house to make their horses jump by nipping at their heels. Austin Davis hello'd the house as was the custom. They could see lights on in several rooms, but you didn't dismount in backcountry and go up to the door. It was a quick way to get a belly full of buckshot. You stayed mounted and called out to the house until you were invited to step down.

Finally Longarm could see a light coming to the door from inside the house. The door opened and a Negro man stood there holding a kerosene lantern in his hand. He raised it until he could see their faces. He said, "What you gennel'mens be wantin'?"

Longarm said, "I'm Deputy U.S. Marshal Custis Long. I'd like to see Mister Dalton Diver. This is an official call."

The servant said, "Why bless you, suh, he be right glad to see you. Ain't had no company all day an' he in heah drinkin' whiskey by hisself and jus' wishin' fo' some company, don't you know. You jes' step on down an' I take you straight in to him. He in de parloah."

Dalton Diver was a ruddy-complexioned man of medium height and weight, though Longarm noted as he got up to greet them that he had powerful-looking shoulders and arms. The top of his head was bald, with just a fringe of light brown hair mixed with gray encircling the rest of his head. He got up from a big leather easy chair to greet them as the servant showed them into the room. There was a small fire burning in a big fireplace, even though the night was not really chilly enough to warrant one.

Diver came forward with his hand outstretched. He was wearing a linen shirt with the collar open and a serge vest and serge pants. His black plantation boots were highly polished, and the chain that hung down from his vest watch fob was gold and heavy. He said in a hearty, welcoming voice, "Come right in, men. Did I hear one of y'all say you was a U.S. marshal?"

Longarm figured him to be five feet nine, maybe ten, shorter than himself. He said, "Yessir, Mister Diver, you did. But it's deputy marshal for both of us. My name is Custis Long and this is, uh, Marshal John Smith."

Dalton shook hands with both of them, and then indicated the sideboard, where there were a number of bottles of whiskey and spirits of different kinds. "What kind of poison will you take?"

Longarm hesitated. He said, "Mister Diver, this is by way of being a official call. You may not want us drinking your whiskey after we get down to our business."

Dalton Diver waved away the thought with an airy movement of his hand. "One ain't got nothing to do with the other. Besides, I couldn't sit here drinkin' alone in front of you, and I'm a man needs a few about this time of the evening." He glanced at the Negro. "Robert, you left your manners outside again. Draw these gentlemen up a chair apiece right close to me so we don't have to yell across the room. Then see what they will have to drink. My goodness, Robert, sometimes I despair of you."

Longarm and Austin Davis waited while the servant put forward two comfortable-looking cloth-covered chairs placed to face Dalton Diver. Then he brought a small table and set it between the chairs. After that he brought a tray and set it on the table. The tray contained glasses and bottles of whiskey, rum, and brandy. There was also an opened box of cigars on the tray. Longarm sat down in the left-hand chair, feeling slightly uncomfortable.

Diver motioned with his glass. "Fill 'em up, gentlemen. Hell, don't keep me waiting."

Austin Davis poured himself a glass of brandy, and Longarm took a little whiskey. Diver said, "Them's good cigars."

Longarm shook his head, and Austin Davis got out one of his little black cigarillos and said, "I reckon I'll have one of these instead."

Dalton raised his glass and said, "To your health."

They went through the motions, mumbling, "And yours, sir." Then they all had a drink. Longarm was pleasantly surprised at the quality of the whiskey. He was regretting taking so little.

Dalton said, "Take a cigar, Marshal. Hell, that's what they are there for."

Austin Davis said, "Mister Diver, you may not enjoy our company so much in a little while."

Dalton Diver had a big, hearty voice. He said, "Then so much the better we enjoy the time while we got it. Marshal, you look like a cigar-and-whiskey man. Quit piddling around with it. If you've got hard work ahead of you, why, it will go better with a good drink of whiskey and a cigar."

Longarm stared at him for a second, and then nodded his head. "Fine. If that's the way you'll have it, so be it." He turned to the table and poured himself a full tumbler of whiskey, and then took one of the cigars, bit off the end, spat the end in his palm, and dumped it into an ashtray.

Dalton Diver winked. "That's the way. You gentlemen don't happen to be hungry, be you? I just got up from the table myself. Got a fine ham and some other good vittles."

Longarm was lighting his cigar, getting it drawing good. But he stopped to answer Diver before Austin Davis could say anything. "No, thanks, sir. We don't want to draw this out any longer than necessary."

Diver settled back in his chair. "Fine, fine. Well, I'm here. What have you come to see me about?"

Longarm took a long drink of whiskey. He said, "I will get to that presently, but I wonder if you might not have a family Bible about. I understand you are a religious man. Most such are in the habit of keeping a family Bible."

Diver nodded. "Yes, sir. Certainly do. Started by my great-grandmother." He motioned with his hand. "Right over there against the shelf of books. On the Bible stand. Thing is too big to hold in your lap. Nearly have to stand up to read it."

Longarm looked over and saw a big book lying open on a wooden stand. He put his cigar in the ashtray, crossed the room, and came around behind the big bible. He saw that it was opened to Isaiah. He didn't know if that was a coincidence or if it had been on Dalton Diver's mind. But it didn't matter to him. He turned the pages of the Bible back to the front, back to where families kept records of births and deaths and marriages and other special events. The first few pages were devoted to relatives of Dalton Diver who were long gone. Finally Longarm found the genealogy for Dalton and his immediate family. Opposite Dalton's name were the names of two wives, and below them the children they had borne. Under the name of Lavinia were ten children, all girls. Hannah's was the sixth name down, and he noted that her full name was Hannah Rose. Her date of birth showed her to be twenty years old.

But it was the children of the other wife, the Shaker wife, that Longarm was interested in. Her name had been Ruth and she had died some six years past. She had had six children, the first two being male. The first was Dalton Diver, Jr., and his birth date would have made him thirty-four years old. The second name was scratched out with a careless pen, but Longarm could just make out the first name of Vincent. He would be thirty years old. The rest of the children on Ruth's side were marked as deceased. But the most interesting thing to Longarm was that Dalton was listed as Wayne Dalton Diver and that he was fifty-four years old. Longarm could not be sure, but it appeared that the second oldest boy, Vincent, had had the middle name of Wayne. He turned away from the Bible, reopening it to its place in Isaiah, and went back to his chair.

Dalton Diver said, "See what you was seeking?"

Longarm took a drink of whiskey and then a draw on his cigar. He nodded. "I would reckon so. I must say, Mister Diver, you look much younger than your fifty-four years."

Diver nodded in receipt of the compliment. "Hard work, Marshal. Hard work and a lot of kids. It will keep you spry having the young ones around."

"You've still got four girls here at home."

Dalton Diver's eyes suddenly got wary. "That's correct, sir. They are upstairs attending to their schoolwork. I believe in an education." He made a wave toward the wall of books. "It's an ignorant man who don't take advantage of the knowledge so many who have come before him have labored to make available."

Longarm looked at the end of his cigar, and took a half a minute to tamp it off carefully in the ashtray. He had the feeling that Austin Davis was about to speak, and he gave him a warning look. When he looked back at Dalton Diver he said, "Mister Diver, I've come to do a little trading with you tonight."

"Horse trading?"

"No, I reckon you'd call it children trading. They ain't children anymore, but they are your progeny."

Diver frowned. "I don't understand you, sir."

"You will presently." Longarm finished the whiskey in his glass and set it on the tray, then leaned forward

154

toward Dalton Diver. "Sir, I've got four of your daughters in jail in town. If you don't do as I ask, I intend to bring federal charges against them."

Diver stared at him for a moment and then chuckled. "Marshal, are you having a little joke with me? They don't put women in jail in this state."

"Maybe not. But they got a women's federal prison, and that is where they will end up. And for quite a long while if I'm any judge."

Diver frowned. "Just what in the hell are you talking about, Marshal? What have my girls done?"

"Between me and you, not a hell of a lot. But I can make a pretty serious case against them for accessory, aiding and abetting, and several other things I can think of, including knowingly harboring a felony fugitive."

Diver stared at him for a moment and then lifted his head. He said in a loud voice, "Robert!"

For a moment Longarm thought he was calling for the servant to throw them out of the house, but when Robert appeared he only said, "My glass is empty. Ain't you ever going to learn your job? My lands!"

Diver waited until the servant had done his work and left the room before leaning toward Longarm. He said, "You mentioned you wanted to trade. For my daughters. What are you asking?"

Longarm said carefully, "Your son, Vince Diver." He let the name hang in the air a moment before he added, "And others."

Diver stared for a long moment. Then he shook his head. "I don't believe I know that name."

"Maybe you know him by another name. Wayne Shaker."

Diver shook his head again. "Don't think so."

Longarm said, "It strikes me as a little arrogant of you, Mister Diver, to choose that particular name. Wayne Shaker. Wayne is part of your name. So is it part of Vince's name."

Diver nodded slowly. "I see why you wanted to look in the family Bible. Don't strike me as playing quite fair."

"And it strikes me as being just a little smug to call Vince, or the head of the gang, by the last name of Shaker, considering that you used to be a Shaker and considering they believe in share and share alike. Is that how you figured to divide up other people's property? Under the Shaker method?"

Diver had a naturally genial countenance, but Longarm could see he was struggling to keep the anger out of it. He said in a stiff tone, "Marshal, by what authority and what right do you come down here interfering in our business and putting innocent women in jail? Where is your power to do that and your power to come here threatening me and bullyragging me into doing your bidding?"

Longarm took the cigar out of his mouth. "Mister Diver, my authority comes from the government of the United States, which charges me with enforcing the law in all its states and territories. My job is to protect the lives and property of the people of the United States, and my right to do it comes from my commission as a police officer, which comes directly from the executive branch of the government, namely the President. So you might say that the President sent me on this thankless job. As for my power to see that right is done, that pretty well comes from the folks in your neighboring counties who are damn sick and tired of your gunmen coming into their towns and robbing and stealing and killing." He sat back in the cloth-covered chair. "As to bullyragging you, well, I ain't seen no sign of that. At least not yet." He glanced at Austin Davis. "You seen me doing any threatening or bullyragging, Marshall Smith?"

Austin Davis said easily, "It appears to me that you've been working your way around to giving Mister

156

Diver a choice. I believe the first thing you said to him on the matter of the business at hand was that you were here to do some trading. I don't see no threat in that.''

Diver stared hard at both of them. Finally he looked away. ''All right. I'm a little overwrought. I made a poor choice of words. However, we are used to settling our disputes among ourselves and not having outside interference.''

It was Austin Davis who answered. ''That's the point, Mister Diver. The differences ain't between yourselves. Your differences are with Llano County and Kimble County and San Saba County, to name a few, and towns like Junction and Llano and Brady and Fredricksburg. Y'all are getting along fine here. But you are bleeding your neighbors dry. The Shaker share-and-share-alike plan might be good for y'all, but your neighbors are going broke sharing with you because ain't none of it coming back.''

Longarm said, ''Look, Mister Diver, I'm going to tell you straight up front what I'm after. And there won't be no use you lying about the affair because I've already got the straight of it. Was you and the banker and the mayor and the sheriff put this deal together. I want some of y'all—though not real bad. Mainly who I want is the hot hands that were pulling the triggers. I don't get them, then there's going to be an awful lot of old men doing some real hard time in prison. Not to mention your daughters.''

Diver sat staring at Longarm while he sipped at his glass of whiskey. Then Diver said, ''I don't know what you're talking about. I ain't got no son and I ain't in cahoots with the banker or the mayor or anybody else about robbing and thieving. I run a little cattle and goat operation and that's the extent of it.''

Longarm stood up. ''All right. Have it your own way. But it is a long trip to visit relatives in prison in Kansas.''

Austin Davis put out a hand to stay him. "Marshal Long, why not be patient with Mister Diver. I think he is at heart a good man. It may be we come at him a little sudden and he's still trying to take it all in."

Ignoring Diver, Longarm said to Austin Davis, "What's to take in? It's a straightforward choice. I'm offering to give him four daughters for one son. Hell, a child in school can understand that. Four for one. You know of a better swap? I'll even throw in about half of what I was going to do to the son in the bargain. Hell, that's four and a half to one. You ain't going to pick up a better day than that, not even on Trades Days with the village idiot."

Austin Davis said to Dalton Diver, "What about it, Mister Diver? It seems to me that the marshal has gone a long way out of his direction to be fair about this. I understand a son is worth more than one daughter. But four of them? And as pretty as they are? Hell, I know what kind of business you been doing on the bride price. And now you can sell all four of them again because they are all widows. And you can thank the marshal for Gus Horne. Actually, his name is Gus White, but you probably knew that. Anyway, it was the marshal made a widder woman out of Hannah and her still a fresh flower."

Dalton Diver opened his mouth, but Longarm spoke before he could get out a word. He said, "Now, Mister Diver, you go ahead and be as stubborn as you want to about this matter. But I do have your daughters and they will go to trial for consorting with known criminals. They . . ."

Diver half rose out of his chair. His face was anguished. He said, "They never *consorted* with them. They was married to 'em, but dammit, they never done no *consortin'* with them."

Longarm said, "That's your story. But the jury that tries them is going to hear a different one. I don't know how much money you got, but you ain't going to have nowhere near as much after you get through paying their legal fees to try and keep them out of prison.''

Austin Davis suddenly stood up. He said in a disgusted voice, "I don't know why you are fooling with him, Marshal. Hell, we got the sheriff. He'll testify against the banker and the mayor. And they damn sure will testify against Mister Diver here. We know damn near everything. What do we want to keep fooling with him for?''

Longarm said, "I'll just take the Bible.''

Dalton Diver stood up to his full height. His mouth worked. He said, "Now wait a minute, wait a damn minute.''

Longarm stabbed a finger at him. "What for? We know the whole plan was yours. Marshal Smith here has seen Vince Diver in Rock Springs and around. He knows his reputation.''

Austin Davis said, "And Dan Hicks.''

Longarm said, "And Jim Squires.'' He shook his head. "Who in hell you trying to fool, old man? We know the whole thing was your idea. Hell, we even know about the paint horse.''

Dalton Diver seemed to collapse. He sat down heavily in his chair and took up his drink, gulping at it. When he lowered it he said dully, "All right. What is it you want? How will you trade?''

"For the truth. I want to know how all this got started.''

Dalton Diver looked resigned. He said, "Then I reckon you better sit down and pour yourself another drink. It takes a little telling.''

Chapter 10

Dalton Diver scratched his ear and said, "You'll have to kind of forgive me, gentlemen, if I get this kind of bass-ackwards and turned around in places. It started better'n two years ago, and like Topsy, it just kind of growed. But you are right about one thing—it had to do with the bride price I was getting on my daughters. But that was just one part. The main part, the robbing part, that started a little bit later, and it wasn't my idea and it wasn't Vince's. It was the banker's, the president of the Mason State Bank, Ernest Crouch. Was him got the biggest part of it started. Though how you figured out about that pinto horse beats me. But then you are federal lawmen, and I reckon they hire fellows like you 'cause you can figure such things out."

Longarm and Austin Davis glanced at each other, both shrugging with their eyes. They both wished Diver would hurry up and tell them what they'd guessed about the paint horse. Longarm had only made reference to it with the idea that it was the horse Vince Diver rode, but Diver had made it sound more complicated than that.

Austin Davis prompted Diver. "Now what about your daughters?"

Dalton Diver rubbed his chin. "Well, I had married

160

off my two oldest daughters and got a pretty good price for 'em. All my daughters is swell-looking girls. Course I didn't get near what I could have got if we'd still been in the Shaker community. But I done about as well as I could around here. Anyway, I was grousing to Vince about it and he said he might think of something. I was just about to marry Sarah, that was the next one, to this Lester Gaskamp feller. Now I knew Vince was doing a little outlaw business, and though I was agin it, I knowed he had to make his way the best he could. Well, he got this Gaskamp feller in with him, and soon as Sarah and him was married, Vince carried him off and got him kilt. So there she was, still an unspoilt flower, and my wife— she was still alive then—said I ought to marry her off again. So I did. Vince found the feller and he had the price and the mayor done the ceremony and she was a widow again."

Longarm stared at him and said, "Now that is one I hadn't heard about. Sarah has been married twice?"

Dalton Diver nodded. "Yeah, but it didn't amount to much. The mayor kind of done it on the run, so to speak, as Vince was taking his bunch over to Brady to rob a cattle buyer they knew had a big chunk of money on him. I don't know how Vince got him kilt, but he managed, and that is the way it kind of started."

Longarm frowned. "I think I need a few more details than that."

Dalton Diver shrugged. "I told you I wouldn't tell it good. Well, you got to go back a little ways and understand that the county was in trouble. Ernest Crouch said that with no more money than was coming in, the bank just wasn't going to make it. You've seen our courthouse, us being the county seat of Mason County. Well, we thought that would bring in quite a bit of business, but it didn't. Mason is nearly the only town of any size in the county, and we ain't got more than two thousand souls even counting Mexicans. Other than that, there ain't another town with more than fifty people in the whole damn place. Besides that, there wasn't no land deals being made or deeds recorded or nothing. No courthouse business. I was talking to Vince about it one day, and he said if the county could guarantee him a safe place to hole up after a robbery, that he'd be willing to split. Take the money right to the bank and give them their share. Well, Ernest Crouch jumped on it like a mockingbird on a June bug. Thought it was a capital idea.''

"And the mayor was already in by this time?"

"Aw, yeah. Fact of the business is, he got in on the marrying the second time he married Sarah. I wish to hell I could think of the name of her second husband. Yeah, the mayor was all for it. Everybody was. Hell, wasn't a soul on the street didn't know what was going on.''

Longarm glanced at Austin Davis and nodded as if to say, "I told you so."

"So we roped in the sheriff and sweetened him up a little. Didn't take much. And that is pretty well the way she got started.''

Longarm frowned. "I still don't understand how you could be sure and get the man on the paint horse, or pinto as you call him, killed.''

Diver was about to speak when Austin Davis said, "Excuse me, Mister Diver. I got a feeling this might go on a little. You made the offer of some vittles a while back. Does that still stand?''

Longarm shot him an irritated glance, but Diver heaved himself up out of his chair. "Oh, hell, yes. Two things we ain't ever been short of, vittles and children. We might as well be sociable about this matter.'' He took a step or two toward a door and hollered, "Robert! Robert! Get in here!'' Then to Longarm and Austin Davis he said, "I'll get Robert to lay out some supper and we'll eat in the kitchen. Be shore and bring your whiskey."

Robert laid out slices of ham with green beans and mashed potatoes and gravy. They did not talk while they ate. Even Diver allowed as how he hadn't quite gotten his fill the first time around and he'd give it another go. But finally they finished. Robert brought cups and the coffeepot, set them on the table, and then left the kitchen.

Longarm said, "Dalton, I still don't understand how you managed to be sure the man you wanted killed would get killed. Did Vince shoot them in the back?"

Diver waved his hand. "Oh, no. Vince would never do nothing like that. Naw, what he done was he sent Dan Hicks in ahead of time to the job. Then when the party rode up Dan done his work. It was good for the place they was robbing. It would make the local law look good. They always taken credit for the kill. Made the folks that was robbed feel like they'd got something in return."

"I see," Longarm said dryly. "But what about the local boys? How come you started using them?"

Dalton Diver shrugged. "Well, hell, they was wanting to marry my daughters too. Only they didn't have no money. So I said to Vince he ought to give the home folks a chance, and he did." He suddenly frowned. "That reminds me about Amos Goustwhite. He owed me some money. He was set on marrying Rebeccah and had been paying a little as he went. They robbed the auction barn and he was on his way over here to give me three hundred dollars when some sonofabitch shot him."

Longarm looked at Austin Davis and smiled grimly. "Yeah, I reckon it was a sonofabitch that shot him. Mister Goustwhite had the bad luck to get in an altercation with Marshal Smith here. Next day he tried to bush-whack him. Didn't work.''

Dalton Diver glanced at Austin Davis and frowned slightly. ''Well, I guess if it was in the line of duty . . . Guess I ain't got no complaint.''

Longarm said, ''But that don't explain Gus Horne, or Gus White. I killed him, and he had some of that score from the auction barn robbery on him. How come he didn't get killed right after he married Hannah?''

Dalton Diver paused to pour some whiskey in his cup. ''Well, that was a kind of strange circumstance. They was heading for the town of Miles to do a robbery when Gus got throwed by his horse and broke a leg. A nearby family took him in and he was laid up quite a spell. I told Vince I needed more money from Gus on account of the delay. Hell, I could have had Hannah married twice more in the time he was laying up. So Vince let him in on that auction robbery. You say he was going to Hannah when you killed him?''

''He was right in the middle of the river.''

Diver shook his head. ''Well that just wasn't right. He should have come by here and paid what he owed before he went near her. And he knew it too.''

Austin Davis said, ''I don't understand Vince robbing the auction barn. That involved a lot of folks from Mason. I would expect that stirred up a hornet's nest.''

Diver made a face and shook his head. ''That was all Vince's doing. I done my best to talk him out of it, but he wouldn't have it. He had it in for Ownsby, and the man is dead lucky he wasn't in that office when Vince walked in to rob it. And I mean *dead* lucky.''

''What did Vince have against Ownsby?''

''Well, I'll tell you. Some few months back Vince carried a bunch of horses to the barn and wanted to sell them. Ownsby said they was stolen and he wouldn't touch the deal. Well, of course they was stolen. Every damn one of them had a different brand. Man acted like he didn't know what was going on. The upshot of it was he took the horses and notified their rightful owners. Made Vince good and mad, I can tell you that.''

Austin Davis said, "Nobody was killed there. In fact, the lady claimed it was Vince riding the paint.''

Diver nodded. "Yeah, he done that. He didn't want everybody getting on to the fact that that was a hearse horse. So sometimes, when it was a short haul and nobody to be left behind, either him or Dan Hicks would ride the horse.''

"Which brings up something I don't understand, Mister Diver.'' Longarm took a moment to figure out what he wanted to ask. "You only had four daughters getting married. But there were a lot more men got killed on the jobs than just them.''

Diver nodded vigorously. "Yessir, and that is a fact and one I'm more than just a little proud of. See, word was getting around about what a good thing Vince and Dan had going. So some of them border ruffians got to insisting they be brought in on the jobs. Well, Vince seen he couldn't refuse them without raising hard feelings. So he took 'em in—one at a time. Naturally, they got to ride the pinto. Wasn't long before them trashy felons wasn't so all-fired interested in joining up. I figure we done the whole country a good service by ridding it of some mighty undesirable folks. Wouldn't you say that was a fact?''

Longarm glanced away and shook his head. He said, "Mister Diver, some of your reasoning just gets right on by me.''

"Yeah,'' Austin Davis said. "What about this Jim Squires? He married one of your daughters, and I'd bet you horseshoes to half-dollars he ain't dead.''

Diver's face suddenly went beet red. He pointed an outraged finger at Austin Davis and said, "Now there, if there ever was a case called for law work, he is one! I let that young villain marry my daughter Salome without payin' the full bride price. Put half down. The understanding was he was to go off on a job and bring me the balance of the money, but that hellion never even meant to stick to his bargain. Right after the marriage ceremony the gang took off for Fredricksburg, and that scalawag peeled off from the bunch and hurried right back to Salome and went to dipping his biscuit in the gravy! Now, tell me *that* ain't crooked! An' I ain't got my money yet. That damn fool daughter of mine up and fell in love with the fool, and I might as well consider her just a dead loss. I've complained about it to Vince, but he just laughs. Now, if you are here to bring justice to this affair, I'd like to commend your eyesight to that bit of thievery!''

Longarm and Austin Davis tried to keep straight faces, but it was hard going. Longarm cleared his throat and said, ''Mister Diver, let's get back to this other business. I take it that some of this money was being brought back to the county. Other than what was given you for your daughters, how did the county get any good out of the robbery proceeds?''

''Why, through the bank. I thought you was on to that.''

''How did that work?''

''Well, Vince give Ernest Crouch part of every job, and Crouch put it in the bank and then distributed it around the county by making loans.'' He shifted his eyes around as if to keep from being overheard and said furtively, ''Though I got to tell you there has been more than a little dissatisfaction on that score. Lot of folks think Crouch has been charging some mighty high interest rates, up to eight percent. It's left some ranchers and farmers where all they can do is pay off the interest, let alone touch the principal on their loans. But I reckon costly money is better than no money at all, which is what we had before this scheme got started.''

"How much has Vince turned over to the bank so far?"

Diver frowned. "Well, I ain't exactly sure, but Vince says it is somewhere about fifty thousand dollars."

"Is that half of what the bunch has robbed and stole?"

Diver gave him a sly wink. "If you was Ernest Crouch asking me, I'd say yes, because that was the deal as was struck in return for Vince and the boys having a safe haven. But I know my own son. If you was to hold my feet to the fire, I'd say Vince give the bank closer to a third."

Longarm stared at the man a moment, took a sip of his coffee, and then glanced at Austin Davis. Davis shrugged. "I ain't got no more questions."

Diver said, "That's pretty much all I know, Marshal. Only question is, what will you give me for it?"

Longarm sat thinking for a moment. He said, "How long will it take you to get in touch with Vince, Mister Diver?"

Diver shook his head dismissively. "An hour at most. He stays pretty close round here. All I got to do is give a note to Robert and, unless he's out hooting and hollering, he'll be along Johnny quick."

"Today is Monday. I want his bunch to rob the Mason State Bank on Wednesday morning at nine o'clock. I believe that is when the bank opens."

Diver stared at him for a moment, horrified. "Rob our own bank? Hell, that don't make no sense. I'll never be able to convince my boy of that."

Longarm took a drink of coffee. "Explain it to him this way. Tell him it's a way of throwing the law off the track. Tell him there are a couple of federal marshals nosing around and they are coming to the conclusion that the gang is part of Mason County. Tell him that a robbery of the bank, especially with that pinto horse right up front identifying them, would make the mar-

167

shals think that the gang ain't Mason County grown. Tell him it would take a lot of the pressure off.''

Diver looked worried. "I don't know about that." He rubbed his chin. "Vince might see the sense in that, but it would upset the hell out of Ernest Crouch. He wouldn't take kindly to having his bank robbed."

Longarm said, "They ain't actually going to rob it, Mister Diver. But it will look like they have. Tell Mister Crouch it will make it very convenient for him to fix up his books for the bank examiners."

Diver still looked dubious. "What are *them*?"

"Mister Crouch will know. And I guarantee you he will think it is a good idea, especially if no money leaves his bank but he can claim he was robbed of twenty-five or thirty thousand. I would imagine that will fill in a lot of holes he's got in his accounting."

Diver looked thoughtful. He said to a far corner of the kitchen, "What are you aiming on doing, Marshal?"

"I've told you from the very first that my main intent is the gunhands, the hot triggers. That includes your son, Mister Diver, along with the rest of them. Dan Hicks, Jim Squires, the other Goustwhite brother." He looked at Austin Davis. "Who am I leaving out?"

Davis shrugged. "We need to make a list there's so damn many of them. And they keep switching around."

Longarm said, "What I want is as many men as your son can round up coming in to rob that bank Wednesday morning."

"You going to gun them?"

Longarm shook his head. "No. I will have it so arranged that they won't have a chance. There will not be a shot fired unless they force it."

Diver let out a long breath. "You shore ask a lot. Man turn in his own son."

"You want your daughters back, Mister Diver? You want to rot in jail with them? You don't cooperate with me, you will get twenty-five years for conspiracy."

It startled Diver. "At my age? Hell, Marshal, at my age I can't do no twenty-five years."

Longarm said steadily, "Then you'll just have to do the best part of it you can, Mister Diver."

Dalton Diver grimaced and squirmed in his chair. "I never expected nothing like this. I don't know if Vince will do it."

"You better see to it that he does," Longarm said warningly. "If you give this away, to Vince or to anybody, you will go to jail along with the banker, the mayor, and your girls. And I will bring in a half-dozen more deputy marshals to scour this area until we bring your son and his gang in. You had better listen to me, Mister Diver. Your son is going one of two places. He is either going to prison or he is going six feet under. And that is not a promise, not a threat, that is a guarantee."

Austin Davis said, "Better go along with Marshal Long, Mister Diver. Prison is better than dead. Men have been known to escape. As long as he is alive there is hope."

Diver rubbed his face again, looking worried. "I don't know, I just don't know. I don't see how I can lie to my own boy. My face will give me away."

Longarm stood up. "That's up to you, Mister Diver, how you do it. You do it my way and I will release your girls and see that you get off pretty light, maybe mighty light. You try and pull something, like telling Vince all about it and maybe trying to break your daughters out of jail, well, it will get pretty bad. You tell the banker or the mayor, well, it will get pretty bad. Your best chance is to go along with what I'm willing to do."

Austin Davis stood up alongside Longarm. He said, "Mister Diver, what it comes down to is that you can wiggle, but you can't get off the hook. Wrong has been done here, and your son is in the big middle of it."

Longarm said, "Mister Diver, I will see order and law

brought back to this county. You can bet your best horse on that."

Diver stood up. He seemed somehow smaller than he had been. "It's a hard thing you gentlemen ask."

Longarm said grimly, "Your son is caught. He is caught right now. You want him dead or alive?"

Diver hung his head.

Longarm said, "He better come in Wednesday morning with his gang, and he better come in no wiser than he is now. I'm obliged to you for the drinks and cigars and vittles."

Diver nodded. "You are more than welcome." He sighed. "Well, when all the cattle are counted, I reckon you'd have to say he done wrong and now has come the time to pay."

"That's it," Longarm said. "You keep thinking like that and you'll be all right."

Diver walked them out to the porch. His voice was mournful and worried as he said, "Is that it? Ain't there no other way?"

"Not that I can think of, Mister Diver."

"I just hate to see it happen in town. Couldn't we all meet someplace?"

Longarm shook his head. "I need them in one place, in one bunch, and at the same time." He didn't add that he also wanted them in the act of committing a robbery.

Diver shook his head. "It's a terrible bad thing you are asking me to do, Marshal."

Longarm was swinging up on his horse. He said, "It was some terrible bad things your son did. Him and the others. And that includes you. Good night, Mister Diver. If you don't keep your word about all of this, I will be back and I will be angry."

They rode away leaving the old man standing on the dark porch. Austin Davis said, "It's kind of pitiful. Makes me feel right sorry for him."

Longarm gave him a glance. "Davis, that is the difference between a real law officer and a half-ass bounty hunter. You see the man now and feel sorry for the trouble he's got. I think about the people his son robbed and killed. That's who I feel sorry for.''

It was late when they got back into town. Austin Davis headed for the saloon and the poker game while Longarm went by the jail. Melvin Purliss and one of the deputies were on duty. They reported no trouble. The deputy said, ''Not as long as we keep the door closed back to the cells. Open that up and you never heard such a racket in your life.''

''Are they eating?''

Purliss said, ''I guess they eat some. Mostly they save it to throw at us when we go back there.''

''Well, you haven't got any business back there.''

The deputy, the one Longarm thought was Bodenheimer's nephew, said, ''Whyn't you stick yore head in back there, Marshal. They been askin' after you.''

Longarm looked around. He said to the nephew, ''Go get the sheriff. I want all four of you up here night and day. I got reason to believe somebody might try and break them out.''

The nephew had been sitting behind a desk. He said, ''Uncle Otis ain't going to like that much, Marshal.''

Longarm jerked his thumb. ''Get. Before I decide to turn you in with them.''

Purliss said nervously, ''You ain't serious about maybe somebody trying to break them girls out, be you?''

''You mean like Wayne Shaker?''

Purliss said uncertainly, ''Well, yeah, him or they daddy.''

''You just stay awake, Purliss. Leave the thinking to me.''

* * *

171

The next day Longarm did not do much. He got up and ate breakfast and then went back to his room to think. He had lunch with Austin Davis. He asked Davis again if he could shoot. Davis said, "I'll tell you again. I'm alive, ain't I? And I ain't a coward."

Longarm said, "It comes down, really, to just you and me. I wouldn't give you four bits to the dozen for the sheriff and his deputies."

"Purliss don't seem all that bad."

Longarm frowned slightly. "Something about Purliss worries me. He is supposed to have worked as a lawman before, in another town. He said Denton and he named the sheriff, but it didn't sound right. I don't know what it is. Probably nothing."

"Hell, you ain't from Texas. How are you supposed to know who is who?"

Longarm shrugged. "I guess I ain't."

That afternoon he walked into the bank and looked around. It was about as he'd expected it to be, a line of tellers' cages behind a marble counter. He could see offices behind the long counter, and he asked if the president was in. He was told that, yes, Mister Crouch was in but was busy. Would he like to wait? He shook his head and left.

Austin Davis said, "When you going to give the sheriff and his boys the good news about their part?"

"I was going to tell them tonight, but I'm afraid it will interfere with their sleep. The less time they have to worry about it the better. I'll go over early in the morning and get them lined out. I reckon you better come with me. In fact I want you to go over to the courthouse with the sheriff and make sure the mayor is manacled and secured. There's no room in the jail for him or the banker, so we are just going to have to tie them down in their offices. So you make sure about the mayor and I'll tend to the bank president. And be sure and have plenty of ammunition."

"I thought you told ol' Dalton Diver wouldn't be a shot fired."

Longarm gave him a look. "I said *we* wouldn't fire the first shot."

"You playing poker tonight?"

Longarm shook his head. "Naw, and you ain't either. Be just like you to get in a fight and lose, just when I need you. I'm going to rest and think and clean my guns. I recommend you do the same."

Austin Davis whistled. He said, "For a peaceful surrender, you shore act like you're getting ready for a war."

Longarm said, "Being ready is the best way to avoid one."

Chapter 11

The bank was directly across the street from the entrance to the courthouse. It was right next to a cross street. Longarm had stationed Austin Davis at its corner. He had good cover and an open firing field, and was no more than twelve paces from where the bandits should arrive.

Longarm had put Melvin Purliss, armed with a rifle, behind a big pecan tree on the grounds of the courthouse. He was some twenty-five yards from the front of the bank and had specific instructions not to fire unless fired upon.

Sheriff Bodenheimer and his other two deputies had been placed inside the bank, behind the long marble counter where the tellers otherwise would be. Longarm had made sure they were armed with double-barreled shotguns. They were not to fire unless plans went awry and the bandits forced their way into the bank. Then they were to let loose with every shell in their shotguns. In his office, the president of the bank, Ernest Crouch, was manacled to his chair and gagged. During his arrest he had threatened Longarm with every type of lawsuit in the books, and had even claimed he could and would have Longarm's badge. He had been in an apoplectic rage until Longarm had wondered mildly what the bank examiners were going to say about one of his depositors, a Mister Vincent Diver, or as he was sometimes known, Wayne Shaker. After that Crouch had shut up and simply glowered. The rest of the bank employees had been crowded into another office and locked in.

There was a mercantile next door to the bank, and Longarm had set up shop behind some sacks of feed that were out on the boardwalk. He was armed with his two revolvers and his Winchester. Both of his revolvers were .44-caliber Colts, but one of them had a six-inch barrel and the other a nine-inch one. He expected he would be doing his work, if there was any to do, with the nine-inch model. The Winchester was a model 1873 that fired the same cartridge as the revolvers. He calculated he was about fifteen yards from the front of the bank. It was a long pistol shot, but the nine-inch revolver was very accurate up to twenty or twenty-five yards.

Austin Davis had said, "You are setting up here like you are trying to stop a bank robbery rather than an arranged surrender."

Longarm had said dryly, "That's right, Marshal Smith."

"It looks a little to me like you have set this up so that you will be apprehending them in the commission of a robbery."

"That's right, Honest John."

Davis had said the mayor had reacted pretty much like the banker until he had heard the magic words about Vince Diver. "After that he shut up and was as docile as a little lamb."

Longarm had put them all in position by half past eight. They had shooed away the whittlers and spitters, and turned back people from approaching the front of the bank. Now a fair crowd was gathered on the other three sides of the square. They were, Longarm thought, damn fools. Anyone dumb enough to risk catching a bullet just to see a spectacle either led a damn boring life or had gone completely loco.

Austin Davis had offered to bet Longarm fifty dollars that the outlaws never showed up. Longarm had studied on the bet for a moment, and then declined on the grounds that it might bring bad luck. "I don't bet on what the other fellow might do. Especially when I got a lot riding on it already."

He looked at his watch. It was ten to nine. He noted, with satisfaction, that some of the people along the sidewalks were starting to wander off to attend to their own business. He was glad, not only for their sake, but out of fear that they might spook Vince Diver. He could only hope that Dalton Diver had done as he had been directed. If he hadn't, Diver and his son and daughters were going to be the losers. Longarm had meant every word that he had told the man.

At nine o'clock there was still no sign of the bandits. Longarm was beginning to despair, and already thinking of the time-consuming work that would be involved in hunting down the gunmen and bringing them to death or justice.

Then, just as he was thinking that, he saw a party of men suddenly appear on the north road, the road to Llano. They came on, heading straight for the center of town. As they got closer he could see that every one of them had his face covered with either a blue or red bandanna. But more importantly, the man in the lead was riding a paint horse. The hearse horse, as Diver had called it.

Longarm had his six-inch revolver in his holster. The gun with the nine-inch barrel was stuck in his waistband. He pulled it free and cocked the hammer. The feed sacks were only about three feet tall, so he was crouched down in an uncomfortable position.

As the riders came on, he was able to count seven. He wondered if Vince had included any of the county boys. Dalton Diver had said they liked to give the home folks their chance so they'd feel a part of the doings. Well, if they were among the seven, they were going to get a chance to see what federal prison felt like.

The riders came on, pulling their horses down to a walk. Longarm saw them glance toward where Austin Davis was lounging around the corner. He hoped his "deputy" had the good sense to have his rifle out of sight and to look casual.

But other than that they seemed to pay no attention to anyone. Perhaps, Longarm thought, they felt their numbers were great enough to handle any force the town could muster, or maybe they felt like they were among friends. He reckoned the latter was more likely the truth than the former. As they came, he examined the man riding the pinto, guessing that he was Vince Diver. The man was stockier than Longarm would have expected. He also seemed older.

But Longarm had no time for such speculation, for the bandits were suddenly wheeling their mounts straight toward the boardwalk in front of the bank. Longarm tensed his muscles, making ready to rise slightly and advise the men that they were under arrest and that they were to dismount and surrender themselves. But in the instant before he could do so, he heard several rapid shots and the sound of yelling. He saw the horsemen stir and look over their shoulders. He turned his gaze to the right. Melvin Purliss had come out from behind the pecan tree, firing shots into the air from his revolver. The words he was yelling came clear to Longarm's ears: "Run! Run! It's a trap! Run for your lives!"

It was too long a shot for Longarm's revolver, and he was scrambling to pick up his rifle when he heard a single shot ring out. He turned toward Purliss just in time to see the deputy clutch at his chest and fall over backwards. Down the street he could see the barrel of Austin Davis's rifle.

There was no time now. He stood up and yelled at the bandits. "I'm a federal marshal! You are surrounded! Throw up your hands and surrender!"

But instead, they had guns in their hands and were firing in all directions. Longarm ducked down just as a slug whizzed over his head. There was nothing for it now but to fight. He came up over the feed sacks, the Colt revolver out in front of him. The man on the paint horse was wheeling around. As he turned away from the bank, he presented himself full face to Longarm. Longarm squeezed the revolver carefully and fired. He saw the bullet take the man and knock him off the back of his horse. But Longarm had no time to look for there was wild firing from all directions. He saw a man go down, obviously from Austin Davis's gun, but then Longarm was sighting on a man in a red bandanna whose horse was rearing up. The bunch had packed themselves in so close they were having trouble separating. Longarm fired, but the man's horse jumped just as the hammer fell and he saw he'd only hit the robber in the arm. He thumbed the hammer back as the bandit turned toward him, raising his own revolver. Longarm fired an instant before the robber, and the man lurched backwards and then fell off the side of his horse.

The melee was clouded with smoke and dust and noise, but it seemed to Longarm he could still see three bandits atop their wheeling, pitching horses. He was trying to find a target in the confusion when, of an instant, the door of the bank suddenly flew open. Sheriff Bodenheimer filled it, a shotgun in his hand. He was just bringing it up to aim when Longarm saw a flutter of his shirt at his shoulder, and then the sheriff was suddenly whirled around and shoved backward into the bank as if someone had given him a hard push. Longarm turned back to the men in front of the bank. One of the three had disappeared, and the remaining two had freed themselves from the tangle of bodies and riderless horses and were spurring their horses across the street to cut across the courthouse grounds. Longarm shoved his revolver into his waistband and jerked up his rifle. He sighted on the back of the right-hand rider and followed him a few steps before he fired. Nothing happened, and he jacked another shell into the chamber and fired again, taking a quick shot just before the robbers could disappear into the pecan trees. The rider went a few more strides with his horse, and then slipped down the side and went rolling over and over along the edge of the courthouse lawn. The last man disappeared from view, spurring his horse east as fast as he could go. Longarm slowly stood up, the sound of the gunshots still ringing in his ear. It had suddenly gotten very quiet. He thought of the sheriff. He hoped the man wasn't dead. He needed him for a witness. He also wondered what had made him decide to become brave and a law officer all at the same time.

Longarm walked out from behind the feed sacks toward the bodies that lay on the ground. Austin Davis came up just as Longarm stepped off the boardwalk. He said, "Well, so much for a peaceful surrender."

Longarm gritted his teeth. "That damn Melvin Purliss. What did you shoot the bastard for?"

"Did you want a gun at your back? I didn't."

"No, but I would have liked to have roasted that treacherous bastard over some slow coals."

"It's over, Longarm. Forget it."

"Yeah," Longarm said. He knelt down over the dead figure of the stocky man who'd been riding the paint horse. He pulled down the bandanna. He said, "Aw, hell. Look here. It's Old Man Diver. Sonofabitch!"

Austin Davis said, "Damn! He must have come along to make sure it went smooth. Then that bastard Purliss put his two cents worth in."

Longarm straightened up. He looked at Austin Davis. "We didn't have no choice, did we? Could you see where we could have done aught else?"

179

Davis shook his head. "No. They had their guns out. If we hadn't cut down on them, who knows how many of these townspeople would have got shot."

Longarm was about to speak when he became aware of the crowd that was building around them. With hard, flat eyes he spun slowly on his heel, staring at them. The people fell back a step. He said harshly, "Damn you! Get the hell out of here! You all knew about this. You're all crooks. I've a great mind to lock the bunch of you up! Now *move*!"

They found the bodies of Vince Diver and Dan Hicks and a man that Austin Davis guessed to be Emil Goust-white. "Looks like his brother."

"I guess Squires got away."

"Unless he's that one you knocked off his horse over yonder."

Longarm stepped up onto the boardwalk. "I better see about the sheriff."

He went inside the bank and found that his two deputies had the sheriff sitting up in a chair. The man was pale and there was a crimson blotch on his right shoulder, but he looked as if he would live. Longarm said to the deputies, "Dammit, get out there and run that crowd off. And one of you have sense enough to get a doctor over here for the sheriff."

A few of the bank employees were venturing out, and Longarm called for one of them to fetch a bottle of whiskey. "And be damn quick!"

He looked down at the sheriff, a slight grin at his mouth. "Otis, what came over you to suddenly start acting like a sheriff?"

The sheriff looked down. He mumbled, "I don't know, Marshal. I just had this sudden overpowerin' feelin' to do my job."

Longarm laughed without humor. He said, "Otis, first rule of being a good lawman is always be sure you have the advantage over the bandits. There are a lot more of them than us. Stepping into an open doorway in front of a bunch of men with drawn revolvers ain't exactly the best way of getting the advantage.''

"I'll shore keep that in mind, Marshal. If I get me another chance.''

Longarm patted him on the shoulder. "You'll get another chance, Otis. You done yourself a whole lot of good today.''

The next day Longarm and Austin Davis sat at a table in the saloon, each of them nursing a whiskey. Austin said, "Well, looks like that wraps it up. You even got Squires. I wonder who the one was got away.''

Longarm shrugged. "I don't know and I don't care. I reckon these folks are out of business. I feel bad about old Dalton, though. But then, you set out to do rough work, you better expect some to come back your way.''

"The daughters. Hannah say anything to you when you let her out?''

Longarm laughed. "Aw, yeah. She said a bunch. I never knowed a girl that young could know so many words you couldn't print in a newspaper.'' He glanced over at Davis. "I ain't sure that Rebeccah knows you were part of this. That door might still be open.''

Davis nodded. "I had considered having a look inside. See how matters fall out. I don't know how they are going to take it about their daddy getting killed.''

"I think they understood the risks of the business. All of them girls was older than their age. They knew what was going on. They knew all about Vince. They also knew why I locked them up. Hannah told me in no uncertain terms that it was a low-down trick and that the only way she'd ever have me in her bed again was if I was to get back in it.''

Davis smiled. "What's next?''

Longarm pulled a face. "I got to transport the mayor and the banker all the way to Austin and turn them over to a federal court. I expect the court will send down an examiner to have a look at Crouch's books. Ought to be pretty surprising.''

Davis pulled several papers out of his pocket. He said, ''These here are wanted circulars on Hicks and Vince Diver and Squires. I know you popped Squires off but you can't take a reward, so I wondered if you'd just put your John Henry on these and the date and place. There's five hundred dollars a head on each of them.''

Longarm looked at him and then at the pencil in his hand. He said, ''You just noted that I couldn't take a reward because I was a deputy marshal. What the hell you think *you* are? You can put them posters and that pencil away.''

Davis blinked. He said slowly, ''You are joshing me. Say you are joshing me. Don't tell me I went through all this for three dollars a day.''

Longarm nodded. ''That's a fact. You didn't earn it, but I figure you got five days coming. You turn in a voucher, in triplicate, to the headquarters in Colorado, and you ought to get your fifteen dollars in, oh, two or three months.''

Davis sagged back in his chair. ''I don't believe this. You're joshing?''

Longarm gave him a blank look. ''I don't understand, Austin. Where is the carefree, lighthearted man who made fun of me for taking matters too seriously? Where is that devil-may-care lad? What happened to him?''

Austin Davis leaned his head back. ''He got buried under fifteen hundred dollars he didn't get.'' Then he sat forward and laughed ruefully. ''What the hell, I took the job. It ought to have dawned on me you was dying to have the last laugh. Well, have it. But let's have another whiskey.''

''I can't,'' Longarm said. He stood up and took a stub of a pencil out of his pocket. He added, ''Don't never say I never done nothing for you.'' Then, on each of the posters, he wrote his name and his commission and his federal district, and certified that each of the wanted men had been killed by Austin Davis. He put the pencil back in his pocket. "That suit you, Marshal Smith?"

Davis looked at the papers and then up at Longarm. "You didn't have to do that. I made a deal. I'm willing to stick by it."

Longarm laughed. "There was no deal. There ain't no such thing as a provisional deputy marshal. I made that up. Now I got to get going. It's a long drag to Austin." He was turning for the door when Austin Davis stopped him. Longarm said, "What?"

"What's it take to be a federal marshal?"

Longarm gave him a sardonic grin. "Why? You thinking of applying?"

"I might. What does it take?"

Longarm thought for a moment. He said slowly, "Well, first of all you got to get yourself in a frame of mind where you ain't surprised by how mean and low-down people can be, what meanness they can get up to. After that, you got to like to be hungry, thirsty, lonely, shot at, shot at and hit, and do all that for poor pay and no thanks. But the last part is the hardest. You got to make yourself believe you are actually doing some good, changing things." He gave Davis a look. "Sometimes that is real hard to believe."

"You think this town will change now?"

"Sure. For a little while. Until somebody else comes along with a way to make some quick money. I got to go."

Davis got up and came around the table and put out his hand. They shook, and Davis said, "I was just kidding about you being an easy poker player. You ain't. You are one of the toughest I ever run into."

Longarm gave him a crooked smile. He said, "There is one other quality you got to have to be a marshal. You got to be able to tell bullshit a mile off. I'll see you, Austin.'' He walked out of the saloon, giving a little wave as he went through the batwing doors. Right then all he wanted was to go back to Colorado and a few of the comforts even a deputy marshal was allowed to have.

But as he walked toward his horse he had the strangest feeling that he'd be seeing Austin Davis waiting for him in Denver, chomping at the bit to become a federal marshal. The thought made him smile. Here you took a man for a fairly smart fellow, and he turned out to be a damned idiot after all. Longarm looked around as he got to his horse and mounted. He'd done a pretty good job and he knew it. Old Billy Vail might piss and moan about him not cleaning the streets before he left, but he was happy with himself. He began to whistle. It wasn't very tuneful, but it was a whistle.

Watch for

LONGARM AND THE DESERT DAMSEL

206th in the bold LONGARM series
from Jove

Coming in February!

If you enjoyed this book, subscribe now and get...

TWO FREE

A $7.00 VALUE—

If you would like to read more of the very best, most exciting, adventurous, action-packed Westerns being published today, you'll want to subscribe to True Value's Western Home Subscription Service.

Each month the editors of True Value will select the 6 very best Westerns from America's leading publishers for special readers like you. You'll be able to preview these new titles as soon as they are published, *FREE* for ten days with no obligation!

TWO FREE BOOKS

When you subscribe, we'll send you your first month's shipment of the newest and best 6 Westerns for you to preview. With your first shipment, two of these books will be yours as our introductory gift to you absolutely *FREE* (a $7.00 value), regardless of what you decide to do. If

you like them, as much as we think you will, keep all six books but pay for just 4 at the low subscriber rate of just $2.75 each. If you decide to return them, keep 2 of the titles as our gift. No obligation.

Special Subscriber Savings

When you become a True Value subscriber you'll save money several ways. First, all regular monthly selections will be billed at the low subscriber price of just $2.75 each. That's at least a savings of $4.50 each month below the publishers price. Second, there is never any shipping, handling or other hidden charges—*Free home delivery*. What's more there is no minimum number of books you must buy, you may return any selection for full credit and you can cancel your subscription at any time. A TRUE VALUE!

A special offer for people who enjoy reading the best Westerns published today.

WESTERNS!

NO OBLIGATION

Mail the coupon below

To start your subscription and receive 2 FREE WESTERNS, fill out the coupon below and mail it today. We'll send your first shipment which includes 2 FREE BOOKS as soon as we receive it.

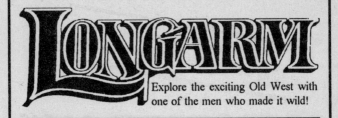